Yule Know It When You See It

A STANDALONE HOLIDAY ROM-COM

Copyright © 2023 by Carly Spade

WWW.CARLYSPADE.COM

Published in the United States by World Tree Publishing, LLC

Cover and Interior Formatting by We Got You Covered Book Design

WWW.WEGOTYOUCOVEREDBOOKDESIGN.COM

A STAND ALONE HOLIDAY ROM-COM

Yule Know It When You See It

CARLY SPADE

A STAND ALONE HOLIDAY ROM COM

YULE KNOW IT
WHEN YOU SEE IT

CARLY SPADE

A STAND ALONE HOLIDAY ROM COM

DEDICATED TO *MY* VIKING.

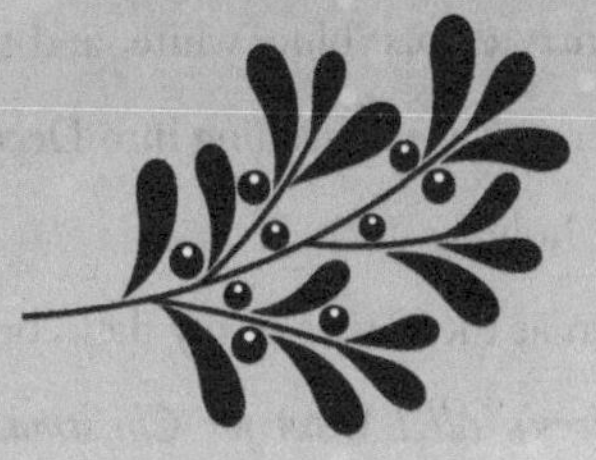

ONE

THEODORA

'TIS THE SEASON to be Mary—Mary McCallister, to be specific. Our office's resident Cheermeister, if Celestial Magazine were, in fact, Whoville. We are not. The irony is never lost on her that she shares the same last name from the starring family of the favorite holiday movie *Home Alone*. I jest, but honestly? We should all be thankful for Mary. If it weren't for her our office would look about as festive as a funeral home every year.

If it were up to our chief editor and reigning She-Dragon, Simone Michaels, we would plop a Christmas tree in the corner and call it a day. No decorations. No tinsel. Just the tree in its naked, natural existence. And this would only be done to satisfy corporate policy. She's our resident holiday Grinch to the extreme. So, as I stare at the bright red-and-green glittering garland bordering my desk in perfect arches, I should feel more gratitude for Mary. Even if that color combination has always made me gag, it's festive. I prefer the more wintry colors: blue, white, and silver. And given Thanksgiving is over, and we're heading into December, it's about time to get into the holiday spirit.

I tap my pink pen at the corner of my desk, bouncing it to the beat of Mariah Carey's *All I Want for Christmas Is You*. A song I'm blatantly sick of, thanks to radio stations playing it when I was growing up, but I can't ever seem to get the tune out of my head this time of year. My teal, ergonomic office chair squeaks as I swivel back and forth. I've written reminders on random Post-Its to call maintenance about that very sound but always get distracted by virtually anything else.

"Hey," a voice chirps in my ear, making the pen fly skyward.

Desiree's chestnut eyes go wide, and she holds her palms at her chest as if I planned to impale her with said pen.

"Des," I blurt her name in a relieved sigh. "You know better than to sneak up on me when I'm 'in the zone.'" Despite their popularity dwindling years ago, I still make air quotes.

"Zone?" Des bats a strand of curly brown hair from her eyes, the black hip-length blazer pulling taut over her biceps as she crosses her arms. "More like I caught you in the middle of a daydream. No one writes romance to that Mariah song any more. And if you *are*, you need to let me proofread before giving it to Simone."

There's zero reason to feel offended by her accusation, given I'm not writing at all, but somehow, I still manage to let it frazzle me.

My spine straightens, and I bob in my seat. "And what if I was?

Mayhaps I'm going for the extra cheese?"

"Uh-huh. Save that for the holiday piece if it's biting at you that much, Theo." Desiree glances at the empty desk several feet from mine that's been vacant for weeks. It never takes this company that long to fill a spot.

"Holiday piece." I snort. "Simone hasn't so much as whispered what she wants me to do. I'm honestly starting to get a bit worried."

As the magazine's resident romance writer, I have the luxury of writing themed short stories every month to fill readers with bubbly heartfelt thoughts. This year's St. Patrick's theme was two star-crossed lovers reconnecting over green beer and Irish jigs in a pub in Pensacola, Florida. The Halloween theme, my second favorite to the holidays, was two people wearing the most ridiculous masks falling for each other before even seeing what the other looked like. Needless to say, I love my job. But the holiday piece is always the biggest draw for the magazine, and my boss has been silent as the grave about it.

"Maybe it has something to do with the new hire replacing the sports columnist," Rupert's voice chimes in as he adjusts his bow tie—a purple one with yellow polka-dots today.

"They finally hired someone?" Desiree asks, sitting on my desk's corner.

Squinting at the bare desk, I immediately imagine who the new hire would be—a tall man. Extremely tall. We're talking over seven feet. Jet black hair. Tanning booth bronzed skin because who in Chicago has a legit tan in the dead of winter? Maybe hazel eyes? And, of course, the straightest, whitest, blinding set of teeth when he smiles.

"Yup." Rupert removes his black circular glasses and clean the lenses with his cardigan sleeve. "They start tomorrow. What do you guys think they'll be like? I only pray, and I do mean *pray*, they'll say more than two words to the rest of us like Lloyd did."

Desiree gasps at the thinly veiled jab against our taciturn former colleague and playfully swats Rupert on the shoulder. He responds with a cheeky smile, like he wants her to do it again. "You got two words out of Lloyd? I swear the most I ever heard from him was 'Mornin'.'"

"Eat your hearts out, ladies, because I got two words and a whole sentence from him." Grinning, I lean back in my chair, interlacing my fingers behind my head.

Rupert's jaw drops, and he sidles beside me, caging me between him and Desiree, seated on my desk. After crossing his legs and resting his chin in his hand, he bats his ridiculously lush eyelashes at me. "Do tell."

Counting on my fingers, I relay the words one by one. "Morning. Hey. And the crème de la crème— 'Mighty cold one today, huh?'"

Rupert slaps his thigh. "Well, hot damn, I'm surprised you didn't propose marriage to him on the spot after those rousing words."

Smiling at the only two people in the office who made the day-to-day bearable for me, I swivel in my chair, deciding the squeaking is now a quirk I'd undoubtedly miss were they to fix it.

"Speaking of crème, I have several desserts to taste at the new bakery on Van Buren Street." Desiree wiggles her brows and swipes a wintergreen Lifesaver I keep in a bowl at the corner of my desk to encourage office-wide oral hygiene.

"Be a little nicer with bakers, hm? I find they're as sweet as their dishes." Rupert elbows me in the arm.

Desiree slides on her peacoat, pulling the hair from its collar. "Oh? And how would you know?"

"Dated a pastry chef. And, I shit you not, he was the sweetest thing I've ever met. Royally sucked when I had to break it off with him." Rupert stares into the distance as if skipping down memory lane and *tsking* once the moment ends.

Dating. Now, there's a word that hasn't left my lips in over a year. But there comes a time when one has to choose between advancing their career and love, right? Both cannot co-exist and receive the same attention. Pure and simple.

After Desiree slips her leather gloves on, she curls a hand over Rupert's shoulder. "Look, pastry chef or not, I can't make any promises. Our readers rely on utter truths. If the cupcakes are bland? I'll say so. If the fritters give me an instant cavity? They'll know about that, too."

"Fair enough," Rupert responds with a shrug. "Not like I'm any less of a viper when it comes to men's fashion."

"And there you go." Desiree smiles, patting Rupert's cheek. She grabs her briefcase, slinging it over one shoulder, and points at me. "We're still meeting tonight for spiked eggnog at The Rooftop, right?"

Groaning, I slump in my seat. "But we *just* got through Thanksgiving."

The Rooftop is our go-to bar because they are a full-service restaurant and have rooftop seating all year around thanks to the dozen outdoor heaters. They make some of the best drinks in the metro area and give a superb view of downtown Chicago to go along with it.

"Your point? Theo, as soon as Black Friday hits, it's game on for Christmas. Everyone knows this." Des arches a brow, staring at me like one would a person who asked why buffalos don't really have wings.

"Fine. I'll be there. Six?"

"Six, indeed. You're welcome to come, Rupert, if you think you can handle not getting sloshed from one drink." Desiree flops a burgundy cap with a stringy ball on top onto her head.

"Thanks, but no thanks. I'd be all about the sloshing if it were Friday night,." Rupert gives an exaggerated hand wave. "You two chicas have fun."

Normally, I don't condone weeknight drinking, but starting this week, The Rooftop sells spiked eggnog drinks for a buck a pop. One simply can't pass that up.

Once Rupert and Desiree leave me to my devices, I place my fingers on the keyboard, staring at the ominous blinking cursor. With each blip, the computer baits, taunts, and otherwise puts me in a trance.

When did Simone plan to tell me what direction I was meant

to go? I can't work like this—not when the magazine expects a particular standard from me. As much freedom as I have to write here, I know freedom is limited to the readers' desires. And I'd made my peace with that. But this?

Growling, I grab one of seven notebooks I keep in my drawers—each a different color and purpose. The one I scoop into my palm is of the yellow variety—my doodling notebook. Opening its pages reveals various sketches and cartoons of nearly everyone who works in the office. Tapping my pen against my lips, I scan the area, settling on Water Cooler Wally. Wally is, for lack of a better term, mysterious. No one knows his precise job within the office, but one thing was certain: ninety percent of the time, you'd catch him leaning on the water cooler, sipping, and striking up conversation.

I draw the rest of the workday away, exaggerating Wally's spiky red hair, the color much lighter than my auburn locks. The water cooler became twice his size, and the poop emoji tie he wore once a week hung to the floor instead of its usual waist length. One glance at the computer monitor blazing at 5:01 PM, and I slam the notebook shut, throwing it in the drawer on top of several bottles of body spray. Pausing, I grab one, nod once, and spritz myself. It's time for the holiday scent: vanilla, cinnamon, and a hint of juniper. Satisfied I will be smelling of Christmas wherever I go, I toss the bottle back home and lock the drawer.

Mary breezes past, clad in one of thirty-odd ugly Christmas sweaters she owns—a cartoon sloth in a red scarf and hat with the words "Merry Slothmas." She trails Simone, who is ignoring Mary, as she gazes from one cell phone to two others.

"Ms. Michaels, I'm sorry. I just wanted to make sure the decorations are alright? It isn't too much?" Mary raises to the balls of her bright red ballet flats, her fingernails picking nervously at each other. Her loose blonde waves bounce before settling over her shoulders.

Simone licks her plump lips, lifting her green eyes for precisely two seconds before returning to her phone. "It's fine. See you tomorrow."

Mary waves to Simone's back, flashing a broad smile that fades into a disappointed frown as Simone exits.

Mary doesn't deserve it. I've never met someone as cheery and kind-hearted as her; she did nothing to deserve Simone's constant cold shoulder, especially when all she sought was approval.

Sliding beside her, I lift my chin, surveying the elaborately decorated office space—a light-up Santa and all of his tiny reindeer, including Rudolph, glittering snowflakes hanging from ceiling tiles, each desk trimmed in garland. And no one could bypass the massive tree she decorated in the corner with a hundred different colored orbed ornaments, turtle doves, tinsel, perfectly coiled silver ribbon, and a shining Bethlehem star on top.

"Mary, you've outdone yourself this year," I say, meaning it.

Mary's face whips to me, tears building in her bright blue eyes. "Really?"

"Are you kidding? I'd have mistaken this place for Santa's

Workshop if I didn't work here." I wink at her, reassuringly squeezing her shoulder before scooping the jacket from my desk chair.

"Thanks, Theo. Honestly. I spent all day on it. Just trying to spread a little Christmas cheer, you know?" She shimmies her shoulders, making the little gold bells on her sweater jingle.

I wrap my black and white checkered scarf around my neck twice and flash her a smile. "And everyone appreciates it, even if they don't voice it."

Mary's grin widens, and she scurries to the tree, making final adjustments.

Spreading a little *Christmas* cheer. Christmas. My favorite holiday out of the entire year, but more for the *feeling* of it. The vibrance that hangs in the air from everyone's nervousness and excitement. The smells sprouting everywhere—cinnamon, cookies, and pine. The music that creates ambiance in every establishment you enter—despite most songs being grossly overplayed. But the "Reason for the Season," the *true* meaning behind Christmas and why I'd done the same traditions every year since I was a child, traditions I was taught growing up, never connected with me.

I've never told a soul about it. Not my best friends. Not even my parents. It was easy enough to go with the flow as I have for the past thirty-three years. Easy to bow my head at the dinner table in prayer, though I'd never really known who I was praying to—I'd simply close my eyes, listen, and mumble "Amen." But I didn't mind keeping quiet because the holidays *are* the most wonderful time of the year. To be specific, spiked eggnog speaks to my soul.

I quickly trek from the office building to The Rooftop only two blocks away, with my hands shoved in my jacket pockets. The crisp air turns my warm breath into swirling smoke, reddening my nose and cheeks. Holiday decorations adorn street lamps and shop windows since the first of November but now hold a sense of wonder I could never appreciate before Thanksgiving—glittering lights at every corner, the chime of the Salvation Army bell, and coins clanking into the collection pot.

I love the holidays.

Desiree had already gotten a table by the time I arrived. The outdoor heaters are set so high that my jacket feels stifling, so I peel it off, draping it over the seat.

"Wow. Right on time. What a rare treat," Desiree says, her tone laced with sarcasm.

"Hardee har," I guffaw, sitting and flicking the drink menu from its center holder.

Desiree leans her forearms on the table, beaming at the decorated trees surrounding us, the Chicago skyline lit in the distance with the seasonal red and green. "I ordered us loaded nachos. Hope that's alright."

"More than alright. I'm positively famished." I gasp. "Ooo. Pumpkin spice eggnog spiked with Bacardi? Yup." Flipping the menu shut, I flutter my fingers. "That was easy."

"You're adorably predictable."

I scrunch my nose at Desiree. "Should I take that as a—"

"Compliment. Yes." Des slaps her palms against the hard surface between us. "So, let's get down to brass tacks. We want to gossip on who the new sports writer will be."

A maroon cocktail napkin resting near my pinky calls to me, and I snatch it, making it into meaningless origami. "I may have already tabulated that in my head."

"Of course you have, *Miss Fiction Writer*."

The waiter approaches our table, young and spry, with such flawless posture it makes me sit straighter. "Ladies, how are we this evening?"

"*We* will be even more fabulous with a couple of those eggnogs," Desiree answers, resting her chin on her folded hands and granting the waiter a sparkling grin.

The waiter smiles back and removes a tablet device from his front black apron pocket. "Fine choice. Which ones would you like? And cold or warm?"

"Warmed? Mm, that sounds divine," I practically groan, clearing my throat from fear of how sensual I sound.

Desiree clucks her tongue against her teeth, staring the clothes right off our waiter before speaking. "I'll have the original eggnog with Amaretto. And my counterpart here will have the pumpkin spice special. Both nice and *warm*."

"You got it. Be back in a jiff." The waiter stays an extra heartbeat, giving Des the hooded come-hither eyes before whisking away.

"Fancy the waiter, do we?" I tease, tossing a ripped part of my napkin at her to snap her back to planet Earth.

She jumps and yelps, batting the napkin away from her face,

"You *are* familiar with my mating rituals. This should come as no surprise. Now—" Des leans back. "Out with it. Who do you envision the new sporty person to be?"

"Well, a guy for one."

"Naturally, as ninety percent of them are. Tall, dark, handsome?"

The skin beneath my eyes crinkles and twitches. "Do I always describe the same dude?"

"More or less. His eyes often change color. Have a type there, Hackett?" Des raises a sculpted brow.

"Who knows what type I have? I think the concept of tall, dark, and handsome is intended to be ingrained in you as a romance author or something."

My eyes grow as wide as Moonpies once I notice the waiter returning with our drinks in handled glass mugs complete with whipped crème, cinnamon sprinkles, and garnished with cinnamon sticks. He rests mine in front of me first, and with Desiree's, he discreetly places a napkin underneath.

"Enjoy," he says to Des, his voice low and husky.

Desiree bites the corner of her lip, watching him walk away and unabashedly checking out his ass.

I scoop the drink into my palms, wrapping my hands around the warm glass. "Phone number on the other side of that?"

Desiree lifts a corner, and her cheeks turn rosy. "Yup."

"You, too, are adorably predictable." I give a playful wink.

"When are you jumping back on the horse? Your 'I'm concentrating on my career this year' excuse has turned into several years. Gotta have a life outside of work, Theo, my dear." Des flashes a coy grin, holding her eggnog with both hands and sipping it.

A deep sigh pushes from my chest, and I trace a circle on the table. "It's not as if I'm closed off to the idea. I've just been out of the loop so long I wouldn't know what to look for."

Desiree's foot bumps mine under the table. "You'll know it when you see it, Theo. *Trust* me."

"That easy, huh?" Sticking my bottom lip out, I scan the patio. "Nope. The love of my life is *not* up here. Can confirm."

Desiree smiles and rolls her eyes. "Okay, brat. Maybe not *that* easy."

"And is Mr. Waiter 'it'?"

She holds the napkin limp between two fingers. "No. He's not. But he *could* be fun for a night or two."

I hold my eggnog up, and we clink glasses.

We spend another couple of hours munching on nachos and enjoying second cups of eggnog, complaining more about the sugar rush over any alcoholic buzz we may be feeling. Desiree texts the waiter before we leave, the two exchanging final glances as we descend the stairs to the main bar area. The vast circular mahogany bar has mostly men seated at the stools surrounding it, sipping mugs and bottles of beer. Dozens of overlapping conversations mix in a cacophony of murmurs and laughter, but one man's voice—deep and gruff—suddenly stands out. I swear he says "fawn" for whatever reason. Strange.

"See you tomorrow," Desiree says, stifling a yawn.

We push our shoulders into the revolving door, parting ways once our feet meet the pavement. While we were in the bar, the temperature dropped to single digits, and for a split second, I regret not owning a vehicle. Then the dead-still traffic, honking horns, and Chicagoans yelling obscenities out their windows remind me why walking a couple of blocks beats driving.

Entering my Michigan Avenue apartment, I toss my keys into the ceramic bowl my baby cousin made for me last Christmas. The sides are uneven, the color a puke green, but she'd made it for me and me alone, so it remains imperfectly perfect in my eyes. I throw my briefcase on the kitchen island with a deep sigh, contemplating watching TV before bed, but deciding it's not worth it. Instead, I go about my nightly routine and slip into a pair of red satin pajamas, another past Christmas gift from my parents. They'd teased that they matched my hair and weren't far off.

After tossing the tanned decorative pillow and two extra white pillows onto the lounge chair facing the windows, I peel back the comforter and yank the pale yellow quilt on top, securing it under my chin. Tomorrow. Tomorrow, Simone will give me my assignment, and I can finally write my favorite piece for the entire year. Until then, I intend to fall asleep with visions of sugar plum fairies and hot nutcrackers dancing in my dreams.

TWO

AXEL

NOT EVERY MAN can pull off a beard—a *real* beard. Hell, some can't even grow a full one. Fortunately for me, I'm not one of those. Call it my Scandinavian blood, but I pride myself on beard maintenance—trimming, shaping, conditioning. And I refuse to walk out of the house if it looks scraggly. This is why I now stand in front of my bathroom mirror, raking oil through it and sliding it across the parallel shaved parts of my head, separating the longer hair slicked back in between.

My best bud Spencer insisted he take me out tonight for a couple of ales to celebrate starting my new job tomorrow: Celestial Magazine's newest sports columnist. It'll be the fourth magazine I've worked for in the States but the first to request *me* to come in for an interview. To say I'd been flattered would be an understatement.

After glancing at myself in the mirror, I snatch my bomber

jacket with furry lining and throw it over a button-down shirt. I slip on a tan knit hat, ensuring it covers my ears, and head out the door. Despite Chicago's brutal winters, it still doesn't compare to Norway, my original stomping grounds. The looks my unzipped jacket garners from folks passing me on the street are borderline amusing. I mean, hey, at least I wear a hat and usually shove my hands in my pockets.

I've lived in several big cities during my ten years in America, but Chicago has quickly become one of my favorites for its skyline alone, especially during the holidays. The buildings seem blanketed in stars with the number of lights they affixed to them. And don't get me started on the marvel that is the giant tree they decorate in Millenium Park. On my first holiday from home, I missed seeing *Julebukk* or Yule goats everywhere, and the town centers morphing into ancient shopping stalls. And the *gløgg*. Damn, what I wouldn't give for a proper glass of mulled wine this time of year. But, alas, any place in America that claims they serve it consistently misses the mark.

The Rooftop bar is only several blocks from my apartment building. When I enter, I immediately slip the hat off and shove it into an inside pocket, dragging my hands repeatedly through my hair. A pair of women sitting at a high-top table pretend not to ogle me, smiling and absently stirring their drinks with a straw. I grin at them and muster a friendly nod.

One thing I love about writing? There is an absolute need to seclude yourself to get the job done. I wouldn't call myself an introvert, but too much socializing has me yearning for a week in a cabin in the middle of nature *alone*.

"Yo, Ax," Spencer calls from the bar, standing on a stool rung to wave me over.

Raising my hand, I signal that I see him before winding through crowded tables. "Hey ya, Spence. How's lawyer life?"

We lock our forearms and give slaps on the back with our free hands.

"Living the dream. What can I say?" Spencer grins and holds his hands at his sides as if the entire world served as his playground. He scratches the stubble on his chin and motions for the bartender.

The heat here resembles roasting in a sauna fully-clothed, and I not only remove my jacket but roll my shirt sleeves as well. I sit in the stool near Spencer and interlace my hands on the bar top. "Still using the job as an excuse for not growing a beard? I know plenty of lawyers with them."

A routine jab between us.

Spencer scoffs. "Not good ones."

"Or maybe you can go straight 'stache." I bob my brows, gaze panning skyward to the hockey game playing on a corner TV— my favorite sport.

Spencer's face appears in my line of vision, blocking my view. "You think I couldn't pull it off?"

"If you managed actually to grow one, I give you two days tops before getting the urge to shave." I smirk and lean back, folding my arms, my shirt pulling tight across my biceps.

Spencer's narrow eyes squint, and he taps a finger on the mahogany. "That a bet, Axel?"

He won't let this go until I bet him. It's often easier to give in to the chaos with him.

"Sure. If I win, you need to wear the "I Like Big Beards and I Cannot Lie" shirt we saw a few weeks ago for twenty-four hours." A snarky smile works its way over my lips.

Spencer rubs his temple but relents. "Fine. And if I win, you gotta wear a Santa hat on Christmas day and show *proof*."

Besides getting a wicked set of hat hair, I don't see how humiliating that's supposed to be.

"Deal."

We shake on it, sealing the agreement just in time for two behemoth-sized beers set in front of us.

"Damn, Spence. Went with the big boys, huh?" Chuckling, I display the size of the mug compared to my forearm which is nearly equal. "This'll do nothing for my Carpal tunnel."

Spence snorts into his mug. "Next, you're going to tell me you got it from typing." He makes a jerking-off gesture with his free hand.

"Nah," I counter, curling my hand around the mug's handle with my left hand. "That's what the left hand is for."

"You're positively disgusting," Spencer jokes, using a horrible version of a British accent.

Smiling and shaking my head, I bring the mug to my lips, relishing in hops and barley. A trait I immediately gave America credit for—they certainly weren't lacking in beer variety.

"Do you do that on purpose?" Spence asks, pointing at my arm.

Quirking a brow, I glance at my bicep stretching the shirt's fabric. "Those are called muscles, Spence. You'd know of them if you did more than just run a bajillion miles a week."

"I could outrun you." Spencer raises his brows over his mug as he drinks.

I chuckle and wipe the beer collecting on the hair above my lip with a cocktail napkin. "Yes, you could. And you can have it."

"Oh. My. God. We love your accent," a high-pitched woman's voice screeches behind us.

"*Faen*," I whisper under my breath, take a long drink, and turn on my stool to face them.

The brunette woman bites her lip and, without shame, roams her gaze from my face to my knees. "Where are you from?"

Condensation from my mug drips onto my thigh, the blonde woman's eyes darting to it.

"The US," I answer, knowing they didn't mean my current residence.

The blonde giggles. "No, we mean where are you from originally with an accent like that?"

"Norway," I clip, raising the ale to my lips and gulping some of it.

The women gasp and swat each other's shoulders, still a barrel of laughs and smiles. I catch Spencer rolling his eyes out of his skull from the corner of my gaze.

"Wow. So, is your name Ragnar or something?" The brunette

asks, inching closer to me, a peculiar lust suddenly playing in her darkened eyes.

I smirk and rest the mug on my knee. "No. Afraid not. Have a cousin named Ragnar, though, and another whose middle name is Thor."

The squealing laughter intensifies, and they grip each other's hands.

I've been in this country for over a decade and have had countless people ask about my accent, that's dwindled since my first year here, but this level of enthusiasm? It's a first.

"Could we—" The blonde starts, removing her phone from the tiniest excuse for a purse I've ever seen. "—get a selfie with you?"

When did being a foreigner become celebrity status?

"Uh," I pause, looking at Spencer for a lifeline.

The asshole looks away.

"Sure," I finish, turning to rest my beer on the bar.

The two women huddle around me, leaning their faces so close to mine that our cheeks almost brush. I spread my arms wide against the bar's edge to appear as if my arms were around *them*.

The blonde raises her phone, framing us, and I debate for a millisecond whether to smile. I don't. Instead, I arch a brow and let the beard steal the show. The shutter goes off not only once but three times, and the blonde lowers the phone, the two of them gazing at the screen as she scrolls through the shots.

"This is perfect. Thank you so much," the blonde exclaims, curling some of her hair over one ear.

"Yes. Thank you," the brunette repeats. As they turn to walk away, she waves at me. "And welcome to America."

I give a forced smile and sigh, returning to face the bar. "They don't ask for my number, don't give me *their* numbers, but ask to take a photo of a damn stranger? I don't get it, Spence."

Spencer has already downed more than half his drink during the entire debacle. He snorts at me. "You're the only guy I know that *complains* about lady attention. And besides, you're acting like you'd do anything with a phone number. Have you gone celibate and failed to mention it to me?"

"It was weird, and you know it," I bark, tilting my head back to chug my drink, all of it, and set the mug back on the bar with only suds remaining. "And why the hell are you talking about celibacy? I still date. Occasionally."

Not that I can recall the last one. Or the one before that.

Spencer clears his throat, finishing the rest and wiping his shirt sleeve across his mouth. He stifles a belch. "Oh yeah? When was the last time you went on one? And what was her name?" Spencer bites his bottom lip, mischief casting in his gaze.

I glare at him, lifting the empty mug to my lips, forgetting I'd finished it. Committed now, I continue to "sip" from the mug, refusing to answer him.

"That's what I thought." Spencer's hand claps against my back. "Not saying you gotta go out there and find a wife or anything, Ax. Lord knows that's not on my top priority list, but even I, as a lawyer, make the time to socialize outside of your ugly ass and work."

"I want to be you when I grow up. Will you take me under your wing?" I bat my eyelashes and lean against him, pressing a hand to my chest.

Shoving me away, Spencer laughs. "Since when did Vikings become hotter than lawyers, anyhow?"

"Since the tenth century, I believe?"

Spencer punches my arm and points at the empty mugs. "Another round?"

I hold a palm up. "Oh, no. If it weren't my first day tomorrow, I'd never turn down free beer."

Spencer jostles my shoulder. "Oh, come on. How about just a pint?"

"Fine."

I really do hate turning down free beer.

Spencer motions to the bartender, ordering two pints of beer, and leans his elbow on the bar. "Feeling good about the new writing gig?"

"Definitely. It's one of the top eight most popular magazines in the country. Will look great on my resume."

The pints arrive, and we lift them, clinking our glasses together in a cheer.

"Cheers to the new job," Spence says, smiling.

"Thanks. Skål."

We sip.

"Not going to lie, though. Kinda crazy they have you start right around the holidays." Spencer curls his hands around the glass, tracing absent circles in the sweat collecting on it.

"I thought that too. But they have some assignment that needs coverage straight away. Said I could start early if I was willing to take it on."

"Oh, yeah? What is it?"

I shrug, eyes focusing on the hockey game but paying attention to Spencer too. "No idea. Money talks, though."

"Indeed, it does, friend. Indeed, it does."

We drink our pints and talk for another hour before I, much to Spencer's dismay, ask to call it a night. Spencer wins the credit card battle to pay the tab, but *I* win by whipping out cash I know he never carries to cover the tip. We exit the bar, taking in the familiar urban sounds of cars honking, murmurs of overlapping conversations, and faint bells chiming from the holidays. A sudden whiff of vanilla, cinnamon, and something earthy hits my nose like a slap. It's gone no sooner than I'd smelled it. Was the holiday ambiance in full swing already messing with my head?

After parting ways with Spencer and making plans to hang out again, I settle in for the night earlier than usual, determined to make the most of tomorrow. First impressions are everything. The chief editor, Simone Michaels, communicated to me in the interview that the rest of my career at Celestial Magazine would depend on this first day alone.

The following day, I'm up several minutes before my alarm goes off, showering, dressing, and out the door before sunrise. The temperature is just frigid enough to make me zip my jacket.

I make it to the corner coffee station I frequent, smiling at the owner. "Morning, Gary. Pot finished brewing yet?"

"You're in luck, Mr. Axel. Finished about two minutes ago." Gary grins back and flips a paper cup into his palm, filling it with the delicious hot beverage. He hands cup and lid to me, nudging his head at the cream and sugar station beside him. "You have a good day, alright?"

"I intend to," I reply, still smiling as I open a sugar packet to add to my black coffee.

After securing the lid, I slip one hand into my pocket, using the other to sip coffee and warm my bones. I take two steps, and my phone buzzes. Glancing at my smart watch, *Mor* blazing the screen. My mother. I sigh because I regret the conversation we're undoubtedly about to have and swipe to answer.

"*Hei, Mor.* How are you?" I pause at the crosswalk, focusing on the taxi cabs crawling past in rush hour morning traffic.

"Axel, my *sønn*, solstice is right around the corner, and I've not heard a word about when you're coming home."

I lick my lips, immediately regretting it as almost instant chapping starts from the below-zero climate. "*Mor*, I told you about the new writing job, *ja?*"

"*Ja*, you did."

A cabbie lays on their horn for five seconds straight, and wincing, I shove the phone against my jacket to not blast my poor mom's ear out. "It starts today. How good of an impression would it be if I were to ask for vacation already, hm?"

Silence falls over the line, and I stop walking, staring up at the gray clouds for an answer, the faint smell of impending snow filtering the air. "*Mor?*"

"But, Axel, all of your cousins will be here. Your brothers and sister, too. I can count on one hand the number of times you've missed *Jul* with your family."

Of course, most of the family would be there because I was the only one who no longer lived in Norway. My youngest brother lives the next farthest away from home with a two-hour drive.

"I know. I'm going to have to ask your forgiveness for this one. I promise I'll make up for it and be there in spring. We can do all the traditional Ostara celebrations like we did when we were kids, *ja?*"

Please, for all the love in the universe, let her take this bargain. I can't stand to hear my mother disappointed.

I pass a Salvation Army rep chiming a bell and pause to dig in my pocket, tossing what coins I have. It still amazes me that they make money this way for charity in America, given how few people kept physical cash on them anymore.

A puff of air fans my ear from her side. "You promise, Axie?"

A smile edges my lips. "Promise."

"Alright. Springtime it is, then. But what will you do out there in Chicago all by yourself?"

Chuckling, I gaze up at the building numbers to gauge how far I am from the magazine office. "I *do* have friends, *Mor*."

"Of course, you do *hånddukke*. You give me a call at least that day, *ja?*"

Puppet. My mother calls me by a nickname I haven't heard since I was twelve. It bubbles something in my chest.

"You know I will. Have a good evening."

She makes kissing sounds. "*Jeg elsker deg.*"

"I love you too." A familiar, warm smile plays on my lips as I hang up, but it soon drops into terror at the sight of the time.

I have precisely five minutes before I'm late when I fully intended to be *early*. Squeezing past a couple walking hand-in-hand in front of me, I sprint down the sidewalk, dodging people like a damn running back in American football. When I reach the building, I'm out of breath and sport a sheen of sweat on my forehead.

Maybe I *should* add a bit more cardio to my workouts. Damn you, Spencer.

I enter the building after collecting my breath and casually move toward the elevator. A woman with auburn hair stands inside, but I'm close enough I can make it before the doors shut. That's until she makes eye contact with me and furiously presses a button.

I rush forward, holding my hand out. "Would you please hold the—"

She fakes an expression like she hasn't been pressing the close button, which resembles mock pity but borderline relief, and the doors thud shut.

I sigh, defeated, and watch the numbers fluctuate for each elevator car, none of which are close to the lobby floor. Glancing at my watch, I let out another sigh. Great. It's my first day on the job and I'm going to be late. All because of a greedy elevator thief.

THREE

THEODORA

I'VE NEVER BEEN late for work. Ever. So, imagine my surprise when I fail to insert the charging cable in on my phone the night before, and it dies. What does this mean? No. Alarm. And I'd love to think I'm the type that has this crazy internal clock situation, wherein I wake up automatically at the same time every morning, but alas, I do not. I'm a night owl. I *hate* mornings despite my forced willingness to face extremely early ones at times to hit a deadline.

So, here I am, sprinting down the street with a donut hanging out of my mouth, only concealer and mascara on my face, and my hair in complete disarray. A street performer unironically plays *Run, Run, Rudolph* on the saxophone, and I let out an actual snarl upon passing him. When my palms fly into the revolving door of the office building, I have precisely two minutes to make it to the elevator and fly through Celestial Magazine's entrance.

"Please let there be an elevator waiting in the lobby. *Please*," I say in silent prayer to myself, my boots thudding against the marble floor, arms poised at my sides to keep myself steady with the occasional slip from wet soles.

Answering my pleas, one of three elevator doors pings open right as I reach them, a man in a trench coat yelling at someone on his cell phone storming out of it. Performing a mental celebration dance in my head, I leap into the elevator, press number seven, and let out a relieved sigh. That's until a man in a knit cap with a Viking beard charges toward *my* elevator with an outstretched hand.

Oh, no. No. No. No. What if he picked a floor below mine? It would add another minute to my already ticking time. Not to mention, I've always hated being stuck in an elevator with only one other person. Talk about unbearable awkwardness.

Quickly, I press the close button, offering him a sympathetic expression even when he asks me to hold the door. At least, I thought it was an apologetic face, but judging by the crease in my forehead, it may have looked more like the need to pass gas. The doors shut, denying him entry, and the last thing I see are his widened Robin's-egg-blue eyes staring at me through the gap.

"Finally," I say through a breath and lean on the back railing, waiting to reach my floor.

I step into the office at 8:00 AM on the dot and feeling pretty damn good about myself, I drop off my coat and briefcase at my desk and make an immediate beeline for the coffee room. Usually,

I'd wait for Bernice to put on a pot, but today, why not? I toss coffee grounds into the filter, check the water is filled to the tippy top, press the brew button, and fold my arms, waiting. The room fills with the aromatic scent of coffee, which never fails to trigger memories of my dad reading the Sunday newspaper and handing me the funnies as a child. The thought makes me smile as I grab a mug from the cabinet, closing the door to see a man passing by with—*a beard*. He's holding a blue knit hat in his hands.

That couldn't be Elevator Guy, could it? I'd only seen him for a few seconds, and the hat made him look different. But then he backpedals to the entryway, pauses, and looks directly at me. There's no mistaking those ridiculously blue eyes. It *is* him.

Crap.

Look busy.

There's a chance he doesn't recognize you and needs a caffeine fix.

Act casual.

I clear my throat and pour coffee into my *Star Wars* Christmas mug—Darth Vader wearing a Santa hat and the words "I Am Your Father Christmas." Grabbing two sugar packets, I rip them open simultaneously and pour them in, trying desperately to ignore the looming shadow suddenly standing beside me.

"You didn't hold the elevator for me." Elevator Guy's voice is beyond deep. It's downright gritty baritone. And it's accented.

I gulp before first looking at him, or rather his *chest*. Lifting my gaze up, up, and further up, I finally look him in the eye. "I have no idea what you're talking about, sir."

"Yes, you do. And I saw you hit the close button repeatedly. Whatever happened to common courtesy?" He points at me with his hat, his stance wide and imposing.

His nose bears a perfect slant, his cheekbones carved like marble, hair a mix between light and medium blonde with both sides shaved, the middle part longer and slicked back. His beard, falling to his collarbones, is perfectly sculpted, brushed, and matches his hair color. And those damn glacial eyes. Why did he have to be so freaking attractive? He is the illegitimate love child of Ragnar Lothbrok from the show *Vikings* and Chris Hemsworth, for crying out loud. If, scientifically, two men could conceive. But seriously, it isn't even *fair*.

"Oh, I remember you now." Playing it cool, I sashay to the fridge, snatching the creamer. "You'd *just* missed the elevator. Tough go, huh? What *you* saw was me pressing the open button. But I couldn't keep those determined doors from closing."

"Really? Because your face suggested otherwise." Those turquoise eyes narrow at me.

After pouring a smidge of creamer into my coffee, putting it back, and snapping a stirring straw into my mug, I brush past him. "Face? Sorry. I make all kinds of faces." I exit the room and head for my desk without letting him continue the conversation.

He *follows* me.

Abruptly, I stop, clutching the mug to my chest. "Why are you following me?"

"Don't flatter yourself. That's my desk. *Right* there." Elevator

Guy points at the vacant desk across from mine.

Arching a brow, I hitch-step toward it, poking a finger against the wood. "This desk. Right here. Is *your* desk?"

"That's right." Elevator Guy plops a briefcase onto it. "Say hello to your new sports writer."

For the love of—why me, world? Why? Not only was I unknowingly cruddy toward a new co-worker, but I also made him late on his *first* day.

"A new writer." A nervous laugh erupts from my chest. "Great. Fabulous."

A brief flash of white shines through his beard as he gives me a lopsided grin. "Any more synonyms you care to add? Terrific, maybe?"

"Prodigious," I blurt.

"Nice one." His eyes do this sexy squinty thing where the corners crinkle and little lines form in the skin below his gaze.

Why does his praise do unmentionable things to my stomach?

Desperate to change the subject, I tap my fingernail against the mug's ceramic. "*You* have an accent."

He begins removing various items from his briefcase, including a basic yellow legal pad, several pens, and a business card holder. "And *you* have ears. *Skål.*"

My nose scrunches, and I have zero time to ask what in the flying hell this means before an intern approaches, holding out a shiny, glistening nameplate to Elevator Guy. "Here you are. Hot off the presses, Mr. Nord."

"Thanks," Mr. Nord replies, resting the nameplate at the front of his desk.

I lean back, squinting at the name printed in bold black lettering. "Axel Nord." An inescapable snort blurts from my nose. "That has to be a pen name."

"It was my grandfather's name." Axel raises both brows at me and presses his fingertips atop the desk, staring me down like a wolf challenging its prey.

I lean even further away, the mug pressed so tightly to my chest that now I can feel the heat seeping through my shirt. "Well, it's a very strong name."

"Thanks?" Axel's gaze shifts away, and he punches his index finger on several buttons of the phone in the desk's corner. His hands are the size of fajita tortillas, and it's a wonder he can manage not to hit more than one number at a time.

I stand there silent and staring like a weirdo.

"You already made me late. Can I set up my desk now and get to work? Or did you want to make fun of my accent or beard next?"

I quite like both of those, to be honest.

"Carry on," I say, lifting my nose and turning away as if he needs my permission.

"Wait," he beckons, waiting for me to look at him. "You know my name. Considering we're co-workers now, care to tell me yours?"

My lips part, ready to answer, but She-Dragon interrupts with a resounding, "Romance, my office. Now."

Simone often refers to her employees by the columns we write versus our actual names. It'd been jarring at first, maybe even a tad degrading, but there were far worse things she could call us.

"Guess my name is Romance. Best to not keep the boss waiting." Grinning at his bewildered face, I turn away and frolic to Simone's office.

Axel mumbles something under his breath in a language I don't understand as I enter Simone's office. She looks extra Queenly today in her crisp burgundy pant suit and jacket ensemble. Her spiky black stilettos are so fierce they could double as concealed weapons.

She points a sepia-toned finger at the door, her perfectly manicured, pointy, burgundy fingernail also questionable as a weapon. "Close the door."

"Yes, ma'am." I shut the door behind me and sit in one of two chairs facing her massive, glossy, black executive desk.

Simone doesn't sit, instead taking a power pose and leaning a hip against her desk. "I assume you've been wondering about your holiday assignment?"

It's consumed me.

"It's crossed my mind a time or two, yes. But figured you'd tell me soon enough." I force a confident smile.

Simone takes a dramatic pause—long enough to cause sweat to bead on my neck. And the worst part? She knows what she's doing. She always does.

"I wanted to wait until the new sports writer started." Simone leans over her desk, snatching a manila folder and holding it out to me.

Blankly, I take the folder and cock my head to one side. "Axel?"

"Who's Axel?"

I open the folder on my lap while blinking up at her. "The uh, the new sports writer."

"Is that his name?" She leans on one arm and runs a finger through the gold chain hanging from her neck. "I like that."

Is my boss getting off over Axel's *name*?

I shake my head, killing the thought as soon as it forms—murdering it. After flipping through several documents and catching glimpses of hockey schedules and locations, I close the folder. "I'm confused. What does my romance column have to do with a sports writer?"

Simone stares past me, rolling her bottom lip past her teeth. She lets her eyes fall shut before lazily opening them and answering me. "I want you to partner with him."

My esophagus detaches from my throat and falls to my feet. "I'm sorry. Partner?"

I've never partnered with anyone at the magazine. Ever. Am I losing my touch? Does she feel I *need* a partner?

"Yes. I want to try something a little different this year." Simone displays her hands like a flashing headline on a billboard. "Holiday Romance in Sports."

My grip tightens on the folder, wrinkling its edges. "I...don't follow."

"Hockey is in season, and I want you and Sports to attend a few games. Interview the players, interview some of the fans. Get a feel for how things change for them and their love lives during the holidays while balancing sports."

I pick the corner of the folder, making small tears. "But how does that create a romance short story? That's what I normally do. Fiction."

"Oh, it'll still be a story. Call it inspiration."

This will surely be the death of me. Or, at the very least, the death of my career.

"Ma'am, I'm sure Axel doesn't know the first thing about romance."

Simone arches a thinly sculpted brow. "You're making assumptions. Besides, that's your department. His task is to keep the sports side of things straight. He's your fact-checker."

I open my mouth to ask what seems the tenth question since she dropped this bomb, but Simone pushes to her feet, pointing at the door and ushering me toward it.

"You have your assignment. Make sure you look at all the documents in the folder and start planning your strategy immediately." She opens the door and motions with her hand for me to exit.

Strategy? Since when does writing romance require a strategy? It's a story with prose, beats, and tone. This also seems fast—too fast to publish this close to Christmas.

"Pardon me saying, Simone, but how do you intend to publish this?"

Simone jerks her head back, almost as if surprised I thought to ask this. "It's going to be an online exclusive this year. If things go well—let's just say I'll fill you in later. Anything else you'd like to question me on?"

"I—" There's no point in arguing with her. In fact, it's a horrible idea ever to try. "Yes, ma'am." Hugging the folder to my chest, I scurry from her office with a new boulder weighing down my shoulders.

"Sports," Simone yells, making eye contact with Axel and nudging her head at her office.

Axel passes me, an unmistakable sense of curiosity wrinkling his forehead. "Should I be worried?"

His sherpa-lined jacket has disappeared, and he stands near me clad in a light gray button-down with long sleeves rolled to his forearms. An intricate colorless tattoo with winding, knotted patterns peeks out, stopping at his wrist but continuing mysteriously further up his arm. How far did it go, I wonder?

Snapping back to attention, hoping he didn't catch me staring, I reply, "She can smell fear."

The expression he gives me is one a person would give to someone who insisted the blunt end of the sword was the lethal end. He shakes his head and is on his way to accept our shared fate. I numbly move to my desk, narrowly missing it when setting the folder down.

"Excuse me?" Desiree appears at my side, her butt pressing to the desk's edge, gaze focusing over my shoulder. "Is *that* the new writer?"

"Why, yes, it is." The words come out far haughtier than I intend, and I type my password with extra zeal, slamming my fingers against the keys.

Desiree holds a brown coffee mug with both hands and stares down the hall. "Jesus," she whispers before sipping her drink.

I flub my password not once, but twice and shriek in annoyance before pressing the backspace button to start over.

"What's your problem?" Rupert asks, catching a final glance at Axel disappearing into Simone's office.

I don't answer Rupert, for I am far too busy stewing in self-pity to produce a coherent sentence.

"That was the new writer," Desiree answers, leaning toward Rupert and nudging her chin in Axel's direction. "I'm taking a wild guess that Theo met him, and she thinks she doesn't like him."

Rupert chews on his thumbnail. "If Theo doesn't like him, I'll certainly take a crack." He feigns fanning himself before turning to face me. "What are the odds he's not straight? Slim, right?"

Finally managing to type my password correctly I access my desktop and open a Word document. "I don't know, Rupert. Why don't you ask him?" My tone is anything but pleasant.

"He certainly has *your* panties in a bind," Rupert counters.

I whip my head around to look at them, only to find both standing there incredulously, raising their brows. "Why are you two looking at me like that?"

"Talk, woman." Desiree grabs the back of my chair and slowly turns me to face them.

In a huff, I sink and fold my arms. "His name is Axel Nord, and yes, that's his birth-given name. He has some accent. Scandinavian, maybe? And Simone is forcing me to work on the holiday writing assignment with *him*."

Rupert blinks his large brown eyes behind his rounded glasses. "I truly don't follow. Why are you in such a hissy fit over this?"

"Because he's an annoying butthole." I nod once for extra confirmation as if *I* need this reassurance. "That's why."

Desiree stirs the spoon in her coffee, making the metal clang against the inside with every other twirl. "You've known him five minutes and have already established him as an irksome orifice?"

Rupert and I both give Desiree similar looks of disgust.

"Such a way with words, Des." I slap my hands on my thighs. "It doesn't take long to rub someone the wrong way when they will *not* get off your back about not holding the elevator for them *one* time. Or when you're trying to make conversation by stating they have an accent, and instead of continuing said conversation by saying where the accent is from, they continue to be sarcastic about it." The words come out in a heated rush, quick, and with little to no breaths in between.

Rupert rubs between my shoulder blades. "Take a breath, sweetie. You're going to pass out."

"Why didn't you hold the elevator for him?" Des lets the spoon handle flop to the rim of her mug and throws her hand to her hip.

Desiree knows I hate being in an elevator with strangers. She's seen me do this on numerous occasions. Why is she trying to rile me up over this?

Me and Desiree share a silent battle of glares before I point between her and Rupert. "Will you both stop grilling me? I've got a ton of paperwork to go through to figure out how even to start this sporty holiday piece, and you guys are cramping my style."

Rupert frowns at me and pats my arm. "Sure we are, sweetie."

"And would you stop calling me sweetie?" I exaggerate batting his hand away.

Rupert presses his palm to his chest. "But I always call you sweetie when you're being a brat."

I gasp, my eyes wide, and try to suppress a laugh.

"Look lively. The Scandinavian doth return." Desiree sucks on her bottom lip, half hiding her face with the coffee mug. She leans her mouth near my ear. "You know, Theo. There is also such a thing as tall, *blonde*, and handsome. Food for thought."

For whatever reason, I clench my butt cheeks at the sight of him. *Clench* them.

"You're meddling, Des," I say through clenched teeth. "Quit it."

Axel rakes a hand through his hair, which, at some point between him entering Simone's office and returning, has gotten tousled out of its sleekness. A single strand hangs over his eyes as he approaches us, his sky-blue gaze panning from Desiree to Rupert and landing on me.

Rupert's throat makes a gurgling sound next to me while Desiree's grip tightens on the coffee mug, causing squeaking sounds against the ceramic.

"Hey, I'm the new sports columnist," Axel starts, extending his hand. "Axel."

Desiree clears her throat before slipping her hand into his. "Desiree." Her eyes bulge at the tattoo encircling his arm.

"Rupert," Rupert butts in, practically hip-checking Desiree. Rupert holds his hand out like royalty, awaiting a kiss upon his ring.

Axel leans away from Rupert's knuckles before awkwardly shaking his hand in the same pose. "Nice to meet you both. The editor told me I'd work with someone on this first piece. Don't suppose any of you can point me in their direction?"

Rising and blocking the nameplate on my desk, I wiggle a pen between two fingers. "Sure. Did she provide their name?"

It's subtle, but Axel zooms his eyes to my knees and back to my face. "Theo Hackett? I assume he works in this same area?"

Desiree sputters a laugh, and I elbow her in the side, keeping a smile plastered in Axel's direction. "Theo, yes, of course. Corner desk. That way." I point to the right.

Rupert slides a hand over his mouth to keep the giggling under control.

Axel's gaze moves between us, initially hesitant, before he crosses one foot over the other. "Alright, I'll go look for him." He doesn't look away, even with his back to us, until he's halfway across the office.

We explode in a fit of laughter and I press a finger to my lips, shushing them *and* myself.

"I've done this prank too many times to count, but this one

seems to be extra satisfying." I flick my hair and sit, pulling myself toward my desk until I'm flush against it.

Desiree gives a final chuckle. "This review isn't going to write itself, but I'll be watching the calamity from across the way." She winks before strolling back to her desk.

"That settles that." Rupert lets out a wistful sigh. "He's bone straight."

"All because he didn't kiss your hand?"

Rupert jostles my shoulders. "Oh, sweetie. Far more than that." After squeezing my bicep, Rupert, too, walks away.

At the back of the office, Axel talks with Mary, who's sporting another Christmas sweater—a green one with a gingerbread man on crutches, missing half of his right leg and the words, "Oh Snap." Mary points in my direction, and when I make eye contact with Axel, he glares at me and storms back to my desk. I pretend to be busy, typing away about absolutely nothing on my keyboard.

Axel clears his throat—*loudly* and picks up my nameplate. "*Theo*dora Hackett."

"That'd be me." I beam at him. "But nobody calls me that except my mom when I'm in trouble."

"Yeah? You in trouble a lot?" He tosses the gold nameplate in his palm, challenging me again with that steely gaze.

I press my palms on my desk. "Are you trying to insinuate I'm a bad girl?"

Of their own accord, my knees pinch together.

"I don't know." He slides the plate back to its home at the front of my desk and makes fists, leaning them on it. His forearm muscles tense and bulge, and it's all I can do not to stare at them. "Are you?"

What is happening? *How* is this happening? And why are my insides swirling because of it?

Extending my hand, I flash a coy grin. "Theo."

Axel drops his gaze to my hand, not shaking it straight away. But when his palm slips against mine, the rough calluses are brushing my skin, and a spark ignites in my core. "Didn't think to tell me that he was a *she*, meaning you?"

I gulp, trying my best not to make it audible. "Watching you make an ass of yourself was far more entertaining."

Our hands had yet to part, both of us still shaking.

"Thanks so much for that." His grip ever so slightly tightens.

Making my eyes form slits, I grip back. "You're *so* welcome."

A deep, throaty, and sexy-as-sin chuckle coils from Axel's chest before he peels my fingers from his hand and steps back. "Since we're going to be working together, we should probably talk things over. But I'm beyond hungry and am near useless without food in my stomach." He cracks his knuckles, pausing to glance at his watch. "So, I'm going to go grab something, and then we'll put our heads together. Yeah?"

If I didn't know any better, I'd say Axel Nord was attempting to take the lead on this little soiree. And I had no intention of letting that happen.

"Perfect. And while you're eating whatever it is you're going to consume, you should come up with a few bullet points on how you plan to cross reference romance with hockey players and fans." I cock my head to one side, still plastering the same coy smile. After pressing the appropriate keys to lock my computer, I push from the desk and snatch my briefcase.

Food *does* sound divine right now.

"Romance?" Axel scratches the back of his head. "You're a romance writer?"

Whew. I'd thrown that quip as a Hail Mary, but Simone didn't disappoint me.

"Did Simone leave out that small detail?" I hoist the briefcase's strap over one shoulder.

"Yes." Axel taps his finger on my desk. "She did."

I shrug without a care in the world. "Like you said. We'll put our heads together."

Bouncing on my heels, I head for the elevator, grinning like the Grinch, knowing the ball is firmly in my court now. And, given it's the third Friday of the month, it also calls for my favorite monthly lunchtime treat: the coveted truffle mushroom sourdough melt. But first, a stop at Desiree's desk to revel in my first of many victories over Mr. Nord.

FOUR

AXEL

I'M A PROFESSIONAL. I've interviewed men nearly twice my size, ready to gouge someone's eyes out, having just lost in the playoffs. But this? Being asked by your editor to team up with someone on a column? And not just anyone, mind you, but a rude, smart ass *romance* writer? It makes me wonder if Simone set up this mystery on purpose. She wouldn't be the first editor I've had who played mind games to entice the best articles from their writers. At any rate, I'll think far more clearly once I put food in my stomach.

Despite the rush I'd been in this morning, I spied a small sandwich and coffee shop in the building's lobby. I hurry from my desk as soon as *Theodora* leaves my company. Theo Hackett. The gall this woman had, knowingly steering me in the wrong direction. But that smug look on her face? I wonder if I'd been the tenth person to fall for it—maybe even the twentieth.

Thankfully, when I reach The Coffee Chapel, there's only one other person in line. Red and green garlands hang from the light fixtures, a miniature tree resting on the counter's corner. A dancing Santa dressed in beach attire but the same trademark red hat swivels its hips in the other corner to the tune of *Jingle Bell Rock*. I press a hand over my growling stomach, its pitch putting the Abominable Snowman to shame. Even more to my favor, the woman in front of me only orders a simple black coffee that arrives in her hand a minute later.

I squint at the boards hanging over the register, rotating sandwich styles written in alternating colored chalk. "The truffle melt sounds delicious. I'll go with that, and a latte if you don't mind." Digging into my back pocket, I produce my wallet.

"You're in luck. We have enough ingredients left for one final truffle sandwich today." The young man behind the counter states. He quirks a brow at my accent but thankfully chooses not to pry.

I chuckle and tap my card against the reader once the total displays. "Maybe I should stop for a lottery ticket too, huh?"

Because getting a final sandwich is about the only form of luck I've had in the past twenty-four hours.

"Here's your coffee. And it'll be just a few minutes to crisp the bread and melt the cheese." The cashier gives a warm smile as he slides the coffee cup in my direction.

"Thanks." I move to the condiment bar, doctoring up my coffee as I see fit and staring out the shop window at the bustling downtown Chicago streets.

Light snow flurries make flakes catch on patrons' hats, jackets, and scarves. A man yanks on his car handle only to find it frozen. I've been there. And my only saving grace had been asking for hot water from a nearby restaurant to thaw it. Tourists mosey from store to store, adding shopping bags to the loads on their arms, gazes almost always skyward. It starkly contrasts to the born and bred Chicagoans who look anywhere but up and keep their walking speed brisk.

"Sir, your sandwich is ready," the cashier announces, and after scooping the brown paper wrapping into my hand, I give a final thank you and move for the exit, spying a redhead stepping to the counter from the corner of my eye.

"Well, that's strange. I don't see my sandwich written on the board. It *is* the third Friday of the month, right? Did I miscount?"

The voice is unmistakable, and I pause at the doorway, freezing like I could become invisible.

"Sorry, Theo, but we sold the last one a few minutes ago," the cashier says.

Smiling to myself, enjoying this upper hand I've suddenly been given, I peel back the paper, and walk back to the counter.

"What?" Theo spats, her hands flying to her hips. "To whom?"

The young man rubs the back of his neck and shrugs. "I'm not sure that's information we're supposed to divulge, ma'am."

"This truffle sauce smells *divine*." My declaration comes out coarse, laced with a sort of prodding challenge.

Theo's petite hands form fists at her sides before she slowly turns on her heel to face me, gaze dropping to the sandwich. Pink flushes her neck and cheeks, her eyes rapidly blinking as she attempts to disguise the internal scream I know thunders within her.

"Axel, that is *my* sandwich." In a huff, she folds her arms.

The audacity of this woman.

Still, I can't deny her attractiveness, especially when she's pissed off. Her button nose tilts higher, cheeks flush with color matching her hair, and those big emerald eyes surge with mischief.

"*Your* sandwich?" I pretend to search it, peeking under part of the bread, flipping it over to observe the bottom. "I don't see your name on it."

A strained smile edges her lips, her thin brows cinching toward each other, and a nervous giggle follows.

I bite my cheek to keep from laughing at how adorably distraught and caught off guard she looks. To further torment her, I toss the sandwich in my palm, raising it with the speed of a tortoise to my lips.

She lurches forward with taut fingers. "That's not what I meant. On this Friday every month, I get that exact truffle sandwich as a treat to myself."

"I see." I sip my coffee and nod. "And you couldn't simply, I don't know, wait until *next* Friday to get it instead?"

"But I—" She stammers, those peat moss eyes as wide as planets. "I have a system. This hiccup will completely throw me off my game."

Well then, we'd be on equal playing ground, sweetheart because the wrench she's become being my partner on a *first* assignment has thrown *me* for one hell of a loop.

I step forward, towering over her like a giraffe with a rabbit. With extreme exaggeration, I open my mouth, watching her nostrils flare, eyes darting to the sandwich. "I may have been inclined to give this to you—" I bite down, tearing the corner and using my tongue to shovel it in, rotating my jaw like a damn steer, chewing, and gulping it down. "But I couldn't keep my mouth from *closing*."

An audible gasp escapes her throat, anger wrinkling her forehead, eyes forming slits. "You won't let that go, will you?"

I dab my beard with a napkin, ensuring no sauce dribbles onto it. "Sure, I will. Because now?" Leaning toward her, I take another bite. "I'd say we're even."

Theo deeply inhales, her jaw tightening at the smell wafting from my sandwich. "You're a butthole."

"I can see this newly formed working relationship going well." A lop-sided grin pulls at my lips, and I raise the sandwich between us. "I'm going to enjoy this at my desk and start reviewing paperwork. Enjoy your BLT, grilled cheese, or there's a McDonald's across the street." I point at the window.

She gives a deranged smile and pageant waves at me, mumbling as I leave, "I hope you choke on a mushroom."

Such holiday spirit.

Back at my desk, I finish the sandwich with one hand, while

scrolling through the hockey game schedules with the other, pausing to jot down dates. The plan is to approach this diplomatically. I'll take the technical sports side of the article, and she'll stick to the fictional. But then, Simone specifically stated this was to be a combined piece. That part still confuses the hell out of me. I ball the paper and toss it in the wastebasket, hitting it off the rim.

"Two points there, slugger," a woman's voice coos behind me.

Peering over my computer monitor reveals a buxom brunette leaning on my desk, the top three buttons of her pink dress shirt showing enough cleavage to be sensual without teetering on sexual harassment.

"Thanks," I clip, moving my eyes back to the screen.

She waltzes around my desk, using two fingers to walk them on the surface, and leans a hip against the wood. "Naomi," she says, extending her hand.

"Nice to meet you. I'm Axel." I quickly shake her hand and return my attention to the schedules though all hopes of concentrating have flown out the window.

She rests one hand in her lap, the other supporting her at her side. "Axel. It certainly matches the accent. Norwegian, right?"

Not many people in America ever guess right. Though all Scandinavian accents sound very different, most say Danish above all else. Sometimes I stop correcting them because it becomes exhausting, and I roll with it.

"Good ear. That's right."

"Confession." She crosses her nylon-covered legs and bends

forward. "I used to go once a year because of a—well, that's neither here nor there, but I had an advantage."

I chuckle and open random windows, scanning the office for anyone witnessing this exchange. "Still. Good ear."

She smiles—endearing and carefree. As if whatever she sets her eyes on is a sure thing. "You have something right here, by the way." She points to the corner of her mouth and then at me.

Swiping a napkin, I dab it and arch a brow at her.

She shakes her head and points at the same spot near her lips. I wipe the other side, and she laughs, holding out her hand. "May I?"

Does she know I can see through her little act like damn cellophane?

I hand her the napkin. "Please."

She leans down, knowingly exposing her cleavage again, using her forearms to highlight her *assets*. After several swipes over my beard, she sits back. "There you go."

"Thanks. I can't tell you how many shirts having a beard has saved, but I can't always feel if something's on it." Smirking, I turn back to the monitor, thinking that was that.

Naomi slides from my desk and pushes a business card under my keyboard. "Pleasure meeting you, Axel. I'm sure we'll see a lot more of each other."

A single dark brow bobs, and like a sliding door, she walks past my desk, revealing Theo standing in front of it with her arms crossed. "You sure work fast. First day, and already making googly eyes at Naomi? Usually takes guys a few days before treading down that particular trail."

I interlace my fingers behind my head and swivel in my chair. "One, I don't make *googly* eyes. Two, she came over *here*, and three, I'm sure these other guys didn't have the Triple Threat."

"As if I even want to ask, but Triple Threat?"

Remaining in my same aloof posture, I flash a wicked grin. "Beard, Blues, and Brogue."

She blinks once, but the corners of her lips quiver, and I swear a hint of a smile appears.

"Brogue is pushing it a little, don't you think?"

Sitting straight, I pluck the pen from my notepad. "Give me a break. I needed something that started with 'b.' It wasn't half bad for making it up on the fly."

Theo smooths her shirt and curls red hair over one ear. "A valiant effort. But I'm still stewing over the sandwich situation."

"The Sandwich Situation," I emphasize, laughing. "That the title of your next romance?"

Her gaze turns glossy, and she whips out her phone, feverishly typing something. "The Sandwich Situation. Enemies to lo—" She clears her throat and slams her thumb against the touch screen several times. "—enemies. Just flat-out enemies."

"Enemies to enemies? What kind of romance is that?" I flip the pen from the inky side to the butt, over and over, needing to keep my hands busy.

"A great one," Theo spats, slipping her phone back into her pocket.

Would it be easier if she *wasn't* cute? Probably.

"Listen, I have an idea. And hear me out before you crap all over it, alright?" I quickly follow up with the second sentence after watching the floodgate she calls a mouth open before I finish.

"Fine." She juts her hip to one side.

Rising, I dig my hands in my pockets and stand near her. "How much do you know about hockey?"

She makes a face like an actor in a mobster movie after saying, "Fuggedaboutit." "Tons. It's my favorite sport."

"Wow." I draw out the "o." "Hope your writing is better than your acting skills."

Her jaw drops.

"Hey, you're the one that lied. Trying to impress me?"

She sucks on her teeth. "Um, no. I don't pretend to like something to get the boy to like *me*, thanks."

"Prove it," I challenge, trying to ignore the tightening in my gut at the sight of her throat bobbing as she gulps. "What's the difference between icing and offside?"

Theo twirls her hair, her spiked heel digging into the tiled flooring as she lifts the ball of her foot. "One is on the top of a...cake?"

There's no denying her adorable mannerisms and the way her wide eyes make her face that much more angelic.

"That's what I thought. If we're going to write this, don't you think you should have a general knowledge of the sport? I have a feeling that's my biggest part in this column, and Simone isn't making that clear."

"Why must I know about infractions to write a romance story?" Theo flicks her wrist in the air.

She knows they're infractions. It's certainly a start.

I shift to the desk's center, leaning back on my hands and gripping the edge. "This is a holiday sports romance laced with real-life encounters we'll use from observing fans and interviewing players and their better halves. Need to step out of your comfort zone for this one, Hackett." Dragging a hand down my face and raking it through my beard, I whisper, "I certainly am."

"I do, maybe, possibly, see your point."

I rest my forearms on my thighs, glinting at her. "Are you telling me you never research things you aren't as familiar with for your pieces?"

"Of course I do. I'm not one of *those* writers. But normally, it entails extensive Google searches. Some of which could be sketchy were I ever on trial for murder."

I don't need to worry about that, right? She wouldn't actually—I let the words fall from my brain as soon as they rise.

"I propose we go to a minor league game first. You can ask all the questions you have. That way, when we get to the major league, we can soak it in and you'll understand the game. Yeah?" I press my fingertips together between my knees.

Theo rubs a lapel between two fingers, her heel swiveling left to right. "Alright. But this *isn't* a date."

What the—

I shoot up like a rocket, fanning my palms at her. "Woah, woah *søta.* Who said anything about a date?"

"It's you and me, alone, in a public place, sitting by each other for hours. It could easily be misconstrued as a date, so I simply wanted to make that perfectly clear." She lets her foot slap back to the floor.

As if the idea of being seen with me in public and anyone assuming we *were* on a date was so—revolting?

Standing, I shove my hands in my pockets and stand in front of her. "The magazine is covering the bill. It's a business trip. And Theo, if I'd been asking you on a date, which I wasn't—" Tilting my chin downward, I lower my voice as I say, "It'd be far more charismatic."

Sudden overlapping smells of cinnamon, vanilla, and something piney float from her skin. That scent. I remember it recently but can't place when. Then again, it's the holidays. Those aromas are *everywhere.*

Theo's bottom lip trembles, and she takes one giant step backward. "When's the game?"

"Tomorrow at seven. The arena is too far to walk, so I'll meet you at the train station at a quarter past six?" I let my eyes roam her expression, body language, and posture. She can take as many steps away from me as she wants, but one thing stands clear: she never turns her *hips* away from me.

"Great. Perfect." Theo snaps her fingers, turns, and scurries away. "See you tomorrow."

Pressing a hip to my desk, I watch her walk, her perfectly rounded ass bouncing. "Exquisite. Sublime," I whisper.

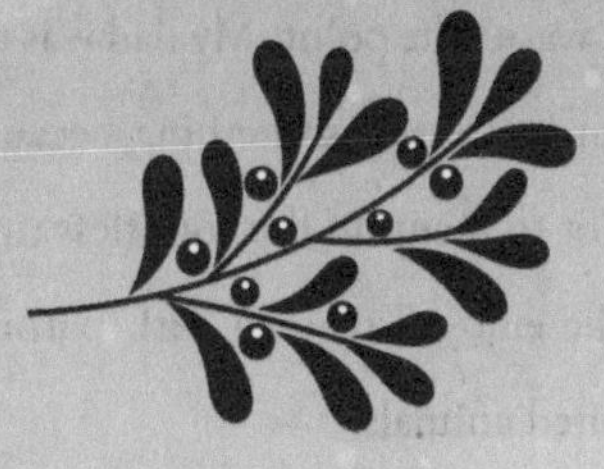

FIVE

THEODORA

HOCKEY: A CONTACT sport played on ice between two teams of six skaters, each attempting to drive a black rubber disc, or puck, into the other's netted goal, past the goalie, with curved sticks.

Did I immediately start researching the daylights out of the sport when I got home last evening? Yes. Yes, I did. Because I'll not have Axel "man-splaining" what's going on the entire time we watch the game. And it's mostly because I don't dare give him the satisfaction. And considering the game wasn't until later tonight, it also gives me all day to continue feeding my brain with all things hockey and watch some highlights.

The only sport I'd been exposed to growing up was football because my dad was obsessed with it, to put mildly. Some of our closest moments had been when I took a keen interest, sprawled on the floor on my tummy with my chin resting on my hands, and watched with him. Did I have any idea how the sport worked? Not really. But that wasn't the point. My dad was the only man for whom I'd ever feign interest in something because I trusted and confided in him. Not to mention the countless times he humored me by pretending he enjoyed playing with Barbies or having tea parties with my stuffed animals.

And you bet your mistletoe I now know the difference between icing and offsides.

Pride swells in my chest as I walk briskly to the train station. Saturday downtown is already busy without adding tourism *and* holiday shopping to the mix. With my gloved hands firmly in my pockets, I keep alert to swerve through the rows of people paying more attention to the skyscrapers than three feet in front of them. I couldn't blame them for being in awe of the Chicago skyline. Aside from New York, it remains one of the most impressive skylines in the world to me. The Sears Tower alone is a marvel. And no, I won't call it the "Willis" Tower. It just sounds plain *wrong*.

I make my way down State Street, pausing in front of the elaborate Macy's window display I hadn't stopped to see yet this year. Some years, they'd focus on toys—a moving train display, animated statues, and dolls. Other years, it would transform into a sneak peek at Santa's workshop, complete with the big guy in his bright red suit surrounded by elves with shoes as pointy as their ears. This year, it features trees and lights in a variety of rainbow colors and toy elves in just elaborate elvish attire hanging from the trees' branches. It's nice to see more than red and green for a change.

Continuing several more blocks, I finally arrive at Millenium Station, spying Axel already standing and waiting on the platform wearing the same bomber jacket and blue knit cap I'd first seen him donning through the elevator doors. He stands out like a burly Viking amidst the patrons surrounding him, both in stature and mere presence. Despite how long he says he's been in America, he looks like a delicious piece of ancient history in modern clothes, trying to blend in with the crowd. And one that can't be less my type. We also work together, which means keeping him at arm's length and not an *inch* closer. At least he makes that part easy with his sarcastic quips and irritating grudges.

Sniffling, I approach him and clear my throat. "The puck."

Axel's scrolling through his phone and pauses, raising those jaybird blue eyes to meet mine. "Did you say fu—"

My hands are at his mouth, pressing over it with widened eyes, a group of kids clamoring past us. "No. Puck. With a 'p.' Like pinecone?"

Axel's gaze drops to my glove, still plastered against his beard, and I snap my hand away. "Did you eat too many Holly berries or something? Why are you spouting random words?"

The genuine perplexed expression melting over his face almost has me laughing. Almost. "The difference between icing and offsides. It has to do with the puck. "Icing" is shooting it from their own side of the center line to the goal without another player touching it. "Offsides" is the attacking team entering the zone before the puck does." I rub my arms and clench my teeth to keep them from chattering.

"Cold?" Axel arches a brow.

Leveling my voice, I cooly reply, "Me? Nope."

He goes quiet and blinks once, twice, and a third time before the skin under one eye twitches. He points at me after slipping his phone into his jacket pocket. "You stayed up until two in the morning researching hockey. Didn't you?"

Guilty as charged.

"*One* in the morning, thank you very much." I cross my arms and rub my biceps, hopping from one booted foot to the other to keep warm while standing in one place on cold concrete.

Axel chuckles and shakes his head, eyes falling on me bouncing around like a roasting chestnut. "You *are* cold."

"Seriously? It's got to be twenty degrees, and we're standing motionless on a cold floor with a *breeze*." I reference his unzipped jacket. "And you're crazy. How are you not shivering?"

Axel's eyes do this sultry hooded thing, and he jabs his thumb at himself. "Norwegian."

Damn. He really *is* a Viking.

An inconvenient *whoosh* swirls in my stomach.

"And that explains the accent. I guessed Scandinavian but didn't want to insult and pretend I knew which country."

An actual warm half-smile graces Axel's lips. "That's refreshing."

"What is?"

"Most people *do* bother to guess because they want to be right. I don't get insulted easily, if ever, but I'm not everybody. It's a matter of respect, you know?" Axel's gaze shifts to the trains on other rails whizzing past as he speaks.

Did we just—have a moment?

Heat rises behind my eyelids and I continue to do my chilly cha-cha dance.

"For crying out loud, Theo. Come on. We can wait in the covered bench area. It'll at least get you out of the wind." Axel motions with his head for me to follow him.

Considering I can't feel my nose, I give in and retreat to the benches, feverishly rubbing my arms once seated. He leans against the partition, crossing his legs at the ankle and smirking at me.

I squint at him with one eye. "I'm surprised you didn't offer me your jacket just to screw with my head."

"Would you have taken it?"

Busted.

"No. I would not have. But it's the principle of the thing, Mr. Nord." Leaning forward, I hug my arms under my thighs.

Axel rakes a single finger through his beard, combing it. "What good would it have done, anyway? All it would do is make *me* cold and leave me standing here in a t-shirt."

"Whatever happened to—" I point at myself and pompously lift my nose. "Norwegian."

"Norwegian. Not inhuman." He tugs my peacoat. "Maybe *you* should invest in a thicker jacket."

I roam my gloved hands over the light gray peacoat with pink plaid lining I've owned for three years. "Perhaps. But this one is *cute.*"

"Of course. Beauty before function, right?" He chuckles, the gray clouds hovering overhead making the blue in his gaze radiate like a sparkling snowflake.

I tip my head. "This is the way."

Axel's head swivels to one side with a quirked brow. "Did you—" A peculiar delight sparks in his gaze. "Was that a *Star Wars* quote?"

No. There'd be no admitting we had something in common. This friendly conversation would lead to more conversation. And this—whatever it was—must remain civil at best. Besides, his smug grin while eating *my* sandwich still taunts my memory like a catchy commercial jingle.

The CTA Holiday Train putters by in the distance, and I spring to my feet, pointing. "Look, there's the holiday train."

Every year, Chicago decorates a train, dubbing it Santa's Express, and covers the entire thing in lights and holiday designs both outside and in. In between cars, Santa and his reindeer greet people waiting on platforms as they travel the stops.

"You ever been on it?" Axel asks, following the train with his gaze as it passes.

"Nope. You?"

He shakes his head curtly. "Nope. But can't deny being curious."

With the holiday train distracting him, I take another look at his face, an *objective* look. Even his side profile is disgustingly handsome and perfect. And I can't help wondering how he keeps his beard so immaculate.

"Taking in the view?" Axel asks, not looking in my direction but giving a sly grin before eyeing me sidelong.

My ears are on fire, and I avert my gaze in time to spot our incoming train. "That's us."

"Saved by a train twice now. How fortunate for you." Axel holds his hand out, motioning for me to go first.

"I haven't the foggiest idea what you speak of, Nord." Tightening my scarf, I brisk past him to the automatic doors.

Heat settles at my back from Axel's chest. "You keep telling yourself that, Hackett."

The doors couldn't open fast enough, and I'm through them and sitting on the first available window seat within seconds. I expect him to sit across from me or in an adjacent row, but much to my disappointment and surprise, Axel sits *directly* next to me.

"What are you doing?" I snap.

"Sitting."

I sit on my hands to warm them. "Yes, but you don't have to sit *right* next to me."

"I don't *have* to do anything." He shrugs one shoulder and slips the cap from his head, dragging a hand through his hair to slick it back.

Gripping the seat with both hands, I flip my hair from my face. "I ride the train solo all the time. I don't need your protection or anything or whatever."

A light chuckle rumbles from Axel's chest. He spreads his giraffe legs wide, a knee brushing mine, and rests his hands on his thighs.

"You ride solo because you *have* to. Today? You don't."

I open my mouth to retort, and virtually nothing comes out. I'm Ariel, the Little Mermaid, and I've lost my voice, only it's been taken from me without contractual agreement.

The train pulls from the platform, and the conductor begins their rounds, traipsing through each car, spotting new passengers to ask for passes or tickets. We hold our corporate-provided lifetime passes when they're near and slouch in our seats to relax the rest of the trip. The silence that falls over us is borderline suffocating. I've never been good at handling idle conversations with people I held tight bonds with, let alone someone new.

As if using the Force to sense my unease, Axel mumbles, "What's your favorite holiday song?"

"*Carol of the Bells*," I answer instinctively.

His eyes are closed, his hands folded, resting on his stomach, but he lazily opens his eyes and gives an inviting smile. "Nice choice. Any particular reason?"

"I don't know. It gives me all the holiday vibes and gets me pumped for the season. Especially the Trans-Siberian Orchestra version." I tap my boots to the familiar beat playing in my head. "And it's neutral. Focuses more on being joyous and grateful versus another retelling of a manger and Three Wise Men."

My neck stiffens, and I don't dare look at him. I didn't come right out and say it, but the implication laced in those words was enough to alert most people.

"So, no *Little Drummer Boy* for you then?"

Shocked he doesn't grill me further on the subject, I whip my gaze to him. He's grinning and casually leaning in his chair with his head resting on the back. "Definitely not in my top ten. What about you?"

"Easy. *Frosty the Snowman*."

I did not expect that.

"Frosty?" I shriek. "But it's so sad. He *dies* in the end."

"No. He *melts*. But I like to believe his spirit lives on." Axel sits straight, his knee bumping against mine as he adjusts.

Ten lords a-leaping suddenly dance in my stomach.

"His—spirit?" My writer's brain dives into the deep end. "Where does it go?"

"Into any other snowman built." A child-like wonder sparks in his eyes. "Another thing I miss about Norway? The powder. Perfect for building snowmen. Here? It gets rock hard overnight, and you're lucky if it doesn't turn black in the same instance."

He's right. Thanks to pollution, vehicles, and below-freezing temperatures. I can't remember the last time I built one myself. And it's not as if I have a front or backyard living in a downtown apartment building. What would Axel look like building a snowman? A guy his size seems somewhat humorous—a dopey smile plastered on his face, snow building up in his beard and eyelashes. The train lurches to a stop, yanking me from my daydream.

"We're here." Axel's rumbly voice announces.

We're off the train and into the arena, waiting in line at the ticket booth. Axel removes his press pass from a jacket pocket, pressing it to the glass partition for the attendant to review.

"Did you need access to the locker room?" The attendant asks, typing away on his keyboard.

Red garland borders each attendant window, and Axel is tall enough it bats him in the eye every time he bends to talk through the speaker. "No. Just seats for the game, please. Put us wherever you want."

And here he goes, retaking the reins. A Viking Chieftain is attending to his peasants—*me*.

The attendant slides two tickets through the window, and I reach in front of Axel, scooping them into my palm for some minor semblance of control.

Axel's gaze goes distant and his hand rubs the back of his neck before thanking the attendant. We make our way to our seats, and the players are on the ice warming up. Some skate past the net, practicing shots, while the goalies do leg stretches.

"Which one is the home team?" I ask.

It feels odd not to take my jacket off indoors, but the coolness from the ice mixed with the frigid temperatures outside forces me to keep my coat on, scarf, hat, and gloves too.

"The white, gold, and maroon jerseys." Axel points, and I faintly make out a growling wolf on the front of one player's jersey.

"Got it." I settle into my seat, ready to give my undivided attention.

Until my stomach growls like a trapped gremlin, reminding me I forgot to eat.

Axel laughs. "You hungry?"

"Nope. No, I am *fine*."

Axel turns to face me, wincing as his leg gets smooshed under one of the armrests. It honestly surprises me he's able to fit in these elf-sized chairs. "They have food. It's not a big deal. I even have the corporate credit card."

A *company* card? What in the flying heck? Why did Simone never feel inclined to give *me* a card? Did she not trust me enough?

"Simone gave you a card? For this assignment?"

Axel's eyebrows squish together and his gaze does that cloudy distant thing again. "Yeah. Doesn't everyone have one?"

My stomach growls again, only this time it has me grimacing from the nausea and hunger pangs eating at my insides.

"Theo, I'm getting you some food." Axel goes to stand.

I yank him back down, or I try. The man is as heavy as three boulders. "Seriously. I'm fine. I want to concentrate on the game."

Slowly, he sits on the seat's edge and dips his face into mine. "Why do you feel basic human functions are a sign of weakness around me?"

A tightness forms in my chest. I *have* been extra quirky around him. But this isn't to say he hasn't lent to the erratic behavior.

"First, it's refusing to admit you're cold. Next, you don't want me sitting next to you on the train. And now, you're *hungry*."

My knee begins to bounce. "It's not about weakness. It's—" I pause and when I meet his gaze, I inwardly crumble just a tiny teensy bit. "—I don't need someone to take care of me."

Because that trust has only ever come back to bite me straight on the butt.

Axel scoffs but still smiles, blonde hair falling over his eyes. "You do know that good guys tend to have it written in their genetic make-up to take care of people, right?"

"Okay, but that doesn't mean you have to feed me."

Amusement sparkles in his gaze. "I wasn't planning on being your cabana boy and feeding you a grape at a time, Theo."

"Do they have popcorn?" Both knees bounce now, and I look away, hating myself for letting him win this one.

"Yes, they do. Several flavors, in fact." He stands and steps back. "You can come with me and carry your own food back to your seat. Deal?"

I give a curt nod and hop to my feet, following him up the stairs and to the food stands in the atrium. We order, he pays with his corporate card, *ugh*, and he goes to grab the popcorn to hand to me but pauses with his hand splayed. Smiling, I take the popcorn with both hands and continue to stuff my face with it as we return to the seats.

The game has already started when we return. I make it through the entirety of the first period without asking a single question. The stern concentration on Axel's face, his eyes following the puck's every move, has me grinning. It's not until the middle of the second period that the home team is scrambling with the puck, struggling to keep it out of enemy hands, before one player lands their stick on it and, backward, launches the puck into the net.

It's the first goal of the game and I'm on my feet, spilling some popcorn and whooping with joy. But no one around me is joining in on the festivities. They are, however, peering at me like a partridge very far from the pear tree. Axel clears his throat and motions with his finger for me to sit.

With the slow descent of an escalator, I find my seat and lean toward him. "What happened? I thought we scored a goal."

"Oh, we did. But we scored against ourselves. The defenseman accidentally shot it into *our* goal." He points to the ice, the home team chastising the player who fudged up.

"But I don't understand. That's our goal, isn't it?"

Axel's shoulder presses to mine, his cologne—musky and vanilla-y—doing obscene things to my stomach. "They switch sides every period. Didn't get to that part in your research?"

"I—" I let my face fall in my hands. "—how embarrassing."

He pats my shoulder and sits back. "Don't worry. I won't let you do that for the Hawks game. Even though I quite enjoy seeing you make an ass of yourself."

My head shoots up, annoyance striking, *blazing,* as I give him my best death-stare. He does that dopey grin before holding my popcorn, what's left of it, out to me. I snatch it from his grasp, slunk in my chair, and don't make a peep for the rest of the game. Unfortunately, the only score made by Chicago would be the one they made for the enemy team, and they finish at four to zip. We don't talk much on the train ride back, but I fall asleep with my head against the window, blissfully helping me avoid making small talk.

The voice announcing our stop jolts me awake, and I wipe the back of my hand at the corner of my mouth.

"No drool," Axel says. "But you snore like a damn freighter."

I gasp. "I do not." My hand is swatting his arm before I can stop myself, and even through the thickness of my leather glove and his jacket, I can feel the bulging hard muscle hidden beneath.

A lump of coal forms in my throat, and I snap my hand to my chest as if his jacket was booby-trapped and rigged with spikes that would strike any moment. Axel's gaze falls to the spot my hand had been, a crinkle forming beneath his eye before he rises, and we exit the train to the empty platform.

"Listen. I know you don't 'need a man's protection,' but it's late. It's Chicago. And as one human to another, I can't in good conscience part ways knowing you're walking home by yourself." Axel shoves his hands in his pockets after flipping the sherpa-lined lapels around his face and zipping the jacket up.

At least Mother Nature gives me a win by becoming cold enough to make Axel Nord chilly.

"I'm not walking." I remove my phone and wiggle the screen at him. "Already called an Uber."

He smirks. "I'll wait with you until it gets here then."

"You honestly don't have to—"

He places a single finger on the tip of my nose. "I don't have to do anything, Theodora."

As innocent and miniscule as it is, the skin-to-skin contact has my chest, neck, and face on fire.

The Uber arrives several minutes later, and before I climb in the backseat, pausing with the door open, I glance at him over my shoulder. "What about you? Rules don't apply to *you* waiting on the platform by yourself?"

Axel waves his phone at me. "My Lyft is a minute away. But I'm flattered by your worries."

His words have my hand wringing the car door frame—worrying over someone leads to other emotions and feelings I'm not ready to have. My writing career is at full tilt, and the last thing I need is a distraction that'd inevitably lead to heartbreak. And a co-worker? Even worse news.

"Worry?" I let out a single "ha" to the sky. "More like looking out for my interests. Given this was for work, you're a liability."

He frowns for a split second as if disappointed by my response before displaying a smile. "You're letting all the cold air into that poor driver's car, Theo."

"I'll see you at work tomorrow," is the last thing I say before flopping into the seat and shutting the door.

As the driver pulls away, I spy in the mirror a giant Norwegian man standing alone with his hands in his pockets, head tilted downward, watching the car until we disappear from view.

SIX

AXEL

THEODORA HACKETT—IS an enigma. She's a paradox of mixed signals, cute mannerisms, and enough back-and-forth commentary that my head is spinning. Just when I think she may be warming up to me, she denies my good manners. And it's not as if I can easily stop what my mom ingrained in me since childhood. But I also didn't want Theo to feel anything less for herself and forcibly took a step back.

And this is precisely why I don't date or get invested in a woman. Because this particular *kvinne* has me staring at a blank Word document for the past two hours. I've done nothing at work except swivel in my chair and click a pen nearly a thousand times. Distractions never help anyone, *especially* writers. It doesn't help that I can also *see* said woman because her desk is ten feet away and she's been equally productive. Instead of typing, she's been writing in a yellow notebook for the past hour and has stolen a glance at me seven times.

On the eighth time, we lock gazes. Her spine straightens, and using her heels, she slowly turns her chair, so her back is to me. Slamming the pen on the desk, I bolt from my chair, taking the long way around the office to get to Theo's desk to peek at what she's been writing. Call me curious. Call me deranged. This woman had me feeling all of it. And honestly? I question whether I should be *feeling* anything at all.

I remain laser-focused on Theo as I weave between desks, glancing only long enough in front of me to avoid colliding with someone passing by. Theo stays with her back turned to my desk until risking a glance over her shoulder and bouncing in her seat when she notices me missing. When she starts scanning the office, I duck behind the water cooler. A man stands there casually, drinking from a paper cup with his other hand shoved in his pocket.

"How you doing?" The man smiles and nods, raising the cup. "Name's Wally. You new? Don't recognize you."

"Yeah," I start, my tone sounding far too distracted to my liking. "Axel. New sports writer."

The nostrils of Wally's wide nose flare wide, and he nods again. "Ah. The replacement for Lloyd. He was a peculiar one. Not very social. Never saw him over here once, come to think of it." Wally shrugs and fills his cup with more water by pressing the cooler's handle.

"Yeah. I'll uh—" Spying Theo writing in her notebook again,

eyes cast downward, I pat Wally on the shoulder. "—I'll try to be better about that. Have a good one."

Wally offers a thin-lipped smile, raising the cup to me again, and I'm back to my stealthy circling of the office.

"Axel. Axel Nord, right?" A high-pitched woman's voice asks.

Pausing, I let my shoulders slump, whispering, "*Helvete*," to myself before turning around. Standing there is a petite woman with bright blonde waves and sporting a blue and black sweater with Christmas tree lights, two squirrels busily chewing on the wires. "Yes?"

With a brightened smile to rival a moonbeam, she sticks her hand out. "I'm Mary. Office receptionist."

I shake her hand but start to side-step us so that my back is in Theo's direction. "Nice to meet you. Can I help you with something?"

"I wanted to give you this since you're new." Mary produces a postcard.

Taking it from her, I arch a brow at the elaborate holiday designs—a red square in the center surrounded by holly and evergreen branches with intertwining lights. Inside the square reads: **Office Christmas Party. Friday at 6 PM until???**

"Office party, huh? This usually a big deal?" I shove the invitation in my back pants pocket.

"Oh, yes. I pull out all the stops and haven't had any employee complaints. I hope you'll be there?" She blinks her big blue eyes and cocks her head to one side.

"Sure," I reply, not remembering when the Hawks game is and hoping I haven't committed to something I can't uphold.

"Great," Mary chirps, clapping her hands together. "I'll let you get back to work, but glad to have you on board, Axel."

"Thanks," I mumble, continuing my office skirting.

Naomi slides in front of me, an arm draped over her chest, fingers twirling her dark hair. "Axel." She frowns. "You still haven't texted me."

And I have zero intention of ever contacting her outside of the office. Zero. I don't have what one would call a direct "type" when it comes to women, but one thing is sure—it's *not* Naomi.

"You noticed that, huh?" I cross my arms.

Naomi blinks, obviously a bit shell-shocked by my response. "Is there a particular reason? Did you lose my number? I can write it down again."

"Naomi," I start, leaning forward to ensure she hears me. "I'm not interested."

Her arms fall slack at her sides, her ruby lips parting. "Excuse me? I mean, why?"

Is this the universe's idea of some cruel joke?

"Do you really want to get into particulars? Right here? In the middle of the office?" I swivel my hips and twirl a finger at our surroundings. "I don't owe you an explanation. I'm letting you know upfront—I'm not interested."

Her cheeks turn rosy, and she clucks her tongue against her teeth. "Fine. You're too tall anyway." She sneers at me before finally walking away.

Definitely *not* my type.

Finally, I make it to Theo's desk undetected and without further interruptions. She's hunched in her chair, busily working away in her notebook. Without announcing my presence, I snatch the notebook.

Theo yelps and leaps from her chair, hands reaching for the notebook I lift above my head. "Axel, give that to me *right* now." She jumps with her arms flailing above her.

I lightly press one hand on her forehead, keeping safe from her unruly limbs. She hadn't been writing at all, but drawing—a doodle of a blonde Viking with the cliché two-horned helmet. "Is this supposed to be—me?"

Theo stops trying to reach for the book and lets out a defeated sigh. "Why would it be *you*?" She lurches forward, hands outstretched, and I effortlessly press a hand to her head again, keeping her away.

"It's a Viking, for one. A blonde one with a beard. He's got a hockey stick instead of a sword and a utility belt with a bunch of pens." I lower the notebook, staring at her.

Did she *doodle* me? And incorporate *symbolism*?

"Your point? Maybe hockey originated in Norway before making it to England." Theo shrugs, eyeing up the notebook before snatching it from me. I let her.

So damn confusing.

"Actually, I think it was Scotland. And that helmet? Cliché

Viking. Historically, they didn't have horns."

Theo slaps the notebook to her desk, doodle side down, and sits, pulling the chair flush with the desk. "Is there something you need, Axel?"

For you to tell me exactly what is or isn't happening between us?

"How much have you written?" I pluck the corner of my phone nestled in my pocket.

She minimizes a window and turns to face me. "Two pages. You?"

"Three."

And now we both lie about work we didn't do? Why?

We glare at each other for several silent heartbeats before my phone buzzes in my pocket. I snatch it, Spencer's face blazing the screen.

"What's up, Spence?" I answer, holding a finger up to Theo and mouthing the words, "I'll be right back."

She mouths, "I don't care."

"Axel, my man. One of the partners won a huge case yesterday, and we're all going for drinks to celebrate. You. Should. Come."

Typically, I'd decline no sooner had the words left Spencer's mouth when in the middle of an assignment. But a night out with the boys to clear my head may be precisely what the doctor prescribed.

"Alright. When?"

"Now."

I pause at my desk, taken aback. "Now? Like right now, now?"

"Right now. Get your blonde ass over here, Ax. The Elephant. State Street."

Thudding my finger against my desk, I attempt to think myself out of it one final time and come up short. "Be there in ten."

After hanging up, I lock my computer and snatch my jacket. No sooner are my arms slipping into the sleeves than I notice Theo perking up, her palms flattening to her desk.

"Where are you going?" Theo asks, her voice gaining an octave.

"Out." I pretend not to pay attention to her as I check my pockets for my wallet and keys.

She leans an elbow on her desk. "Out? On a date?" Theo's left knee bounces ever so slightly.

"I didn't say that." I keep my answers mysterious, having the sudden urge to see if I can somehow make her jealous.

She presses a hand to her thigh, stopping her erratic knee. "But you didn't *not* say it."

"Is it really your concern, Theo?" I move from around my desk, taking two steps in the exit's direction, but stop to peer at her with raised brows.

Theo clears her throat and uses her pen to scratch the back of her head. "No, it is not. I was only curious. You have fun."

"Oh, I plan to." After flashing a wicked grin at her and winking, I walk away, not daring to look back.

I've been at The Elephant with Spencer and his co-workers for the past hour. A satisfying buzz has fogged my brain just enough to melt several cares from my shoulders; hockey plays on three of seven TVs hanging around the establishment, and I've only thought about Theo *once*. Life is good.

"You seem distracted, Ax. And more than your usual writer self." Spencer puffs on a cigar from the stool next to me, sipping a scotch.

I curl my hands around the pint of beer half gone in front of me. "How so?"

"Well, for one, you normally people-watch, and you haven't so much as scanned others at the bar. And you keep drifting into the distance." He holds the cigar with his teeth.

"Lot on my mind with the new place and writing assignment is all." I swig back the rest of my beer and motion at the bartender for another.

Spencer leans on the bar and taps my arm, coaxing me to look at him. "You remember that I'm a lawyer, correct? It's my job to read people. What aren't you telling me?"

That I'm equally irritated and intrigued by my new co-worker?

"Oh, come on. How many more shots you plan to miss, Malone?" I yell at the TV.

"Axel," Spencer barks. "How's the new assignment? Is this what it's about?"

Sighing, I hold my head low, knowing he will *not* let this go until I confess everything. "The new assignment is fine. It's a holiday sports romance piece."

Spencer laughs and douses his cigar in the ashtray. When I don't so much as crack a smile, he frowns. "Wait. You're serious. Romance? You?"

"The editor paired me with another writer. *She* writes romance stories for the magazine." I snatch the new glass of beer as soon as it lands on the bar.

Spencer flags the bartender before he walks away. "Can we get two shots of Jack, please?"

"Why did what I said make you order shots, Spence?" A flash of red hair peeks between bodies on the other side of the bar, and my spine tingles.

The woman turns, laughing, her eyes not green, but brown. Her nose slants downward, not tilted up like—I interrupt my thought, ashamed I somehow got excited at the prospect of *her* inexplicably being here, as if it would've been a serendipitous sign or something.

"Because this is clearly about a woman." Spence nudges my arm and hands me the shot glass filled with amber liquid. "Take your medicine, and then tell me everything."

We tap glasses, then the bar, and down the whiskey.

I flick my glass away, not wincing at the burn coursing my throat, and comb my beard with three fingers. "My partner, this woman, we've butted heads from day one. And we keep doing this cat-and-mouse routine that's bound to drive me insane."

"You sure about that? Sounds like you kind of dig it, my friend."

Spencer chuckles and drums his fingers on the bar.

I turn in my stool to face him, a cinch forming on my forehead. "Dig it? Why would I enjoy arguing with someone?"

"It's not arguing." Spence closes his eyes and vigorously shakes his head. "What *I* do is argue. What you're doing with this woman is called 'banter.'"

Scoffing, I turn my attention to the TV. A commercial for the CTA Holiday Train plays, and it makes my chest tighten. "I don't know, Spence. It started with her irritating me, but after yesterday, I thought I might be starting to like her. But her? Oh, she can't stand me. *Trust* me."

Spencer laughs so hard that he falls off his stool, his hand gripping the bar edge the only thing that keeps him from landing on the floor. "And this is why I know you can't write romance."

"What the hell are you talking about?" I tug him the rest of the way onto his stool with little effort.

"Tell me this. Have you made her laugh? Does she always seem to face her body toward you? Ever catch her staring at you?" Spencer sways slightly, and if it weren't for the truth of his words, I would've blamed it all on the alcohol.

I skirt my tongue along the hair bordering my bottom lip. "Maybe?"

"Uh-huh. She probably likes you, Ax. A lot of women do. But this is the first you seem to like back. At least since 'what's her twat'." Spencer grabs my shoulder and his grip grows so tight it wrinkles my shirt. "I'm so proud of you."

"Knock it off, you drunk." I chuckle and shrug his touch away. "And her name was Caroline."

Spencer flaps his lips. "Caroline. Twat. Sounds all the same to me. She doesn't deserve a name for what she did to you, man."

Royally cheat on me and stole money for extra sting.

"Is she hot?" Spencer bounces his brow, his eyes forming half-lids now.

The way those pants hugged Theo's ass. The spark that springs in her gaze and the crinkles that form near her eyes when she laughs. "Yeah. She is. And a redhead."

Spencer slaps his thigh. "Nice. Look, man—" His arm drapes my shoulders as he pulls me to his side. "—look at the banter as foreplay. And *enjoy* it. Enjoy the journey, my friend."

Nodding, I stare at the golden, bubbly liquid in my pint glass. I've never been as unsure about something as I am with Theo. Not so much her feelings toward me but rather how far I want to try and pursue this. Was it worth the time? The effort? Caroline had been my longest relationship with a woman at a little over two years and look how *that* turned out. So much time had been wasted only for her to rip out my heart and stomp on it. No. I'll enjoy time with Theo whenever she feels compelled to give it to me, and if we become friends? Great. But beyond that? My heart isn't there. It can't be.

Two of Spencer's lawyer pals are behind us, stumbling and patting our backs. They each have a beer bottle in hand, and one lawyer almost drops it when he trips on a stool leg. "What are you two hens cackling about over here? Come play pool. Can't be half as bad as we are right now at it."

Obliging, Spence and I spend the rest of our time there playing pool with the other lawyers. I stopped drinking an hour before I planned to leave and walk home with a dozen thoughts plaguing my brain. I thought the night out would do me good, but it further perplexed me.

My apartment is quiet when I walk in. Living alone without so much as an aquarium in your place tends to be that way. My Yule tree glows bright in the corner, and I stare at the warm lighting, the golden hue calming me. I drag my fingers over the pine cones, fake berries, and fruit hanging from its branches, ornaments I've decorated the traditional yearly tree with since as far back as I can remember. A pile of logs rests near the fireplace—one of the singular aspects of this apartment that sold me. That and the floor-to-ceiling windows overlooking the Chicago skyline.

I crouch near the logs, rummaging through them until I find the one that's shaped the most perfectly of the lot, and toss it in my palm. Taking it to my room, I remove the carving knife from the storage chest at the foot of my bed, hover it above the trash can, and whittle. Traditional Yule logs were not, in fact, cakes like they'd come to be through the ages. Initially, they represented the protection of the home, and every family would burn this specially selected log for all twelve days of Yule. And despite no longer living in Norway, I never skipped this crucial aspect.

I carve the uruz, ansuz, and raidho runes into the log—symbols representing strength, prosperity, and growth. The idea behind is that you burn the log toward the end of the year and carve hopes and wills for the new year. What I wouldn't give to share this, any of this, with someone. This time of year has always made me the most homesick when I can't make it back to Norway. And the emptiness has already settled in, with the solstice still being days away.

After I finish, I rest the log under the tree for safekeeping and pause to stare out the window. There's more to Theo than she lets on, this much is clear. And a deep-rooted part of me wishes she wouldn't put up her guard as much around me. I like the small parts she's let me see, her humor, her creativity, and her obviously closeted inner fangirl for *Star Wars*. But the job comes first. It always has.

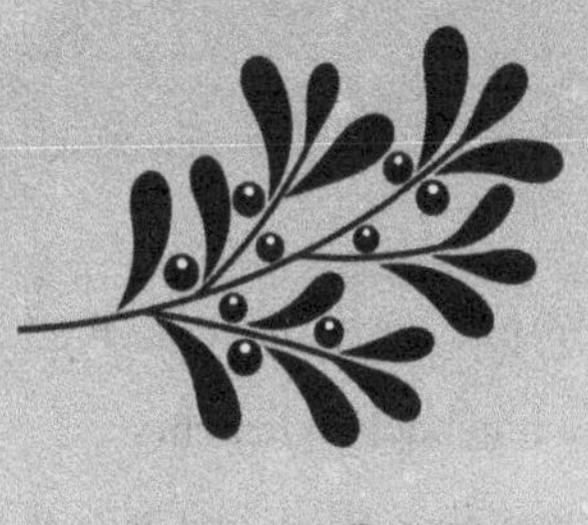

SEVEN

THEODORA

I'M PAINFULLY AWARE that my only semblance of progress on my hockey sports romance thus far is a singular word: hockey. And I'm also disturbingly aware of how many times I've glanced at Axel's empty chair this morning. It's bad enough that when he left on a whim yesterday, I stewed over whether or not it was for a date for far longer than anyone who doesn't care should have. And what's worse? I made up scenarios in my head on how the assumed date went. It mostly involved the woman tossing a drink in Axel's face and leaving mid-dinner or Axel throwing his napkin to the table and reaching across to kiss the ever-loving daylights out of her.

I know. Dramatic. This is why the magazine pays me to write romance, which I should be doing right now. But the afternoon draws near, and Axel is still nowhere to be found. Rubbing my face with both hands, I return to my computer and rest my fingers on the keys.

I whisper to myself as I type, "Hockey, much like sex, is a full-contact sport."

"Wow, a whole opening line. You're on fire." Desiree leans on my desk, clutching a notebook to her chest.

"It's a *great* opening line. That line is half the battle when starting a new story." I lift my chin and over-emphasize hitting the spacebar.

Des pats my head like encouraging a puppy. "Where the hell is Axel?"

"What do you mean?" I pretend his absence not only doesn't bother me but that I've hardly noticed.

Desiree rolls her eyes and turns my chair to face Axel's desk. "He hasn't come in since he left yesterday afternoon."

"Huh. Weird. But I'm not his secretary, so how should I know?"

Desiree's notebook thwacks my arm. "You're full of more shit than the end of the day in a porta potty outside a construction site."

I golf clap. "Prime analogy."

Desiree curtsies as Simone breezes past her, power-walking toward her office. The woman never moseys anywhere because time is most certainly money.

I leap from my chair, my cardigan sticking between the armrest and chair back, yanking me back down. "Simone, ma'am," I call out when she's already three feet from her office by the time I free myself.

"Yes, Romance?" Simone's thumb works quickly across her phone screen, and she doesn't look up.

I'm ecstatic she recognizes me by my voice.

"Do you know where Axel is? He hasn't shown up yet today, and we really need to work on that piece."

"Uh-huh," Desiree says under her breath.

Simone's gaze snaps to mine. "Who?"

"Sports."

"Oh, right." And her eyes are back to her phone. "Didn't he tell you?"

"Tell me—what?" I hesitate to ask for a millisecond, primarily to hide the anxiety and vexation punching at my gut.

"He's at the arena."

Exasperation plagues my very core because she couldn't have meant the *hockey* arena. Right?

"As in, the hockey arena?"

Simone graces me with another glance, but coats it with indignation. "What else would that mean?" Her foot begins to tap, and I have about thirty more seconds before she deems me a waste of her valuable time.

"But I thought the Hawks game is tomorrow?" I rummage through scattered papers on my desk, finding the schedule and noting the date I circled and highlighted.

"Yes, but they *practice* today." Simone turns her back and adds, "You should probably be there too. Don't you think?"

Of course, I should be there. Why hadn't he said anything?

"Yes, ma'am." I jump into action, lock my computer, and slip on my jacket.

"Foodie," Simone shouts from the threshold of her office. "My office."

Desiree does a two-fingered salute and squeezes my bicep as she passes. "Text me, yeah?"

"Sure thing." I smile, grab my purse, and hurry to the train station.

The United Center atrium is completely decked out for the holidays, with tinsel, garland, and lights hanging from every fixture and bordering all windows and doorways. There's a photo booth area for fans to take photos with custom Hawks holiday décor and a small stage where entertainers perform before the puck drops.

No attendants are working the ticket booth, so I approach the only food stand with an employee standing at the register. "Excuse me? Do you need a pass, ticket, or anything to watch practice?"

The older woman with peppered hair pulled into a bun lifts her warm, slightly-sunken eyes to me and smiles. "Nope. It's free. But it doesn't start for another hour or so."

Another hour? Then what the hell is Axel doing here?

"Is there something else going on before then?"

The attendant nods and points toward one of several gate

entrances leading to the arena. "Open skating for the public. You can rent skates from me here if you want to give it a go."

Ice skating. It's been nearly twenty years since I donned blades. Is Axel—*skating*?

"Yes, please. How much?" Digging into my purse, I produce my wallet.

"Five bucks. What size you need, sweetheart?" The woman lowers her head behind the counter.

"Seven, please." I pluck a five-dollar bill from my wallet and hand it to her.

The attendant places a pair of gleaming white skates with brown laces and black scuff marks on the toes and heels from previous wearers. Bright purple guards cover the blades. The laces are tied together, and I drape them from my shoulder just as I had in my youth.

"Thank you." I wave at the attendant before heading through the gate.

When I fully enter the arena, fewer people skate on the ice than I anticipated. A mother holds her young daughter's hands as she fumbles on her skates, a teenage girl makes laps, occasionally turning to skate backward, and there's only one other person— Axel freaking Nord. He doesn't do anything fancy and is simply skating circles on a pair of sport skates, but this isn't a sight I ever imagined in a thousand years I'd see. And more astonishing? Despite the cold temperature here, which has to be even more chilly on the ice, he wears no jacket, only a T-shirt and jeans.

I sit in one of the hundred available stadium seats, taking off my dress shoes and exchanging them for a pair of skates. Doing up the laces, I pat them to ensure they're snug, memories of doing this same action at seven years old flashing through my mind. I move to the open space leading to the ice, pluck off my guards, and wait for Axel to circle back.

Axel spots me and gapes before turning his heels to stop where I stand. "Theo. I was going to call you soon before practice starts to let you know I'm here—" He points behind him. "How *did* you know I was here already?"

His surprise and unease have me beaming inside. And the sight of his bare, muscular arms, that elaborate tattoo making another appearance, and seeing more of it this time? It almost elicits a whimper from my throat.

"Simone told me. Gotta say I didn't expect *this*, however." I step onto the ice.

Axel's hands launch toward me. "Do you know how to—"

"Skate?" I grin and glide over the ice with ease, doing a complete turn with extra flourish before facing him. "You're looking at a two-time youth state figure-skating champion."

Lazily, Axel skates to my side and chuckles. "Well, damn. And here I hoped to see you fall on your ass every five minutes."

"No such luck, Chuck." I dip my head back into a layback spin, circling several times before gracefully pulling out of it. It's like riding a bike. "And are you saying you wouldn't have tried to stop me from falling?"

Axel snickers and speed skates past me, spins, and does a drift stop, sending ice spraying at me. "You don't need my help. Isn't that what you said?"

I had said this, yes. But now, for whatever reason, the idea of his hands on me, even if it was only to keep me from hitting the ice, seems—nice. "Suit yourself." Shrugging, I zoom past him, whisking around the rink's perimeter, using my arms at my sides to guide my movements.

"How did you grow up skating and not know much about hockey? They share the same turf," Axel says with a smirk, yelling this to me when I draw near but keep moving past him.

"I was there to skate, Axel." I glide back to him and come to a grinding halt at his side. "Not to learn hockey."

Axel grins, a devilish mischief playing in his gaze as he spins. "When you skated, was it solo?"

Where is he going with this?

I skate literal circles around him, and he lets me. "Yes. Why?"

Axel's lips take a wicked curl upward before his arm is around my waist, spinning us in circles. My heart throttles in my chest, and it downright stops when he lifts me from the ice for a breath, doing it with such ease one would think I weigh nothing more than a snowflake. He sets me down, still grinning.

"How the—" Breathing has become difficult, and my throat feels like sandpaper. "—how do you know how to do that?"

We're both paused in the center of the ice, the other few skaters continuing laps around us.

"Aside from playing hockey through college, my sister figure skated. When her partner got sick or had to take the day off, she'd rope me into helping her practice." The chill from the ice has turned Axel's nose red, and he sniffles, rubbing a knuckle under it.

A dozen glittering monarchs churn in my stomach at this revelation. I press my hand to my stomach and skate a little closer to his side. "What else you got?"

His face falls, and he cracks his knuckles, sliding his skates forward and backward as if antsy. "You sure?"

"Yeah. Let's just not try any crazy over-the-head moves. We're not exactly at that level of trust yet."

He swivels a nonchalant circle around me. "Yet?"

Rolling my eyes, I push against his chest, sending him skating backward. "You know what I mean."

"Skate backward to me." He makes 'come at me' gestures with his hands and waits.

Whose idea was it to do this again? To put myself in a position where his hands would be *on* me? Mine. All freaking mine. Mental facepalm.

Giving him my back, I glide toward him and can't help the gasp that pushes from my lungs as his hands latch over my hips. He pulls me closer and lifts me straight up before resting me on the ice. His arms wrap around me from behind, and he spins us, lifting, and resting me on the opposite side. His hand dips to my shoulder, causing me to duck my head under his arm, and when I stand upright, I instinctively take his hand.

We lock gazes as we skate hand-in-hand, and electricity sparks through every nerve in my lower body. I've never felt this sort of—connection or reaction—with anyone before Axel, and it drives my mind into treacherous territory. A domain I should have sealed away behind a tightly locked metal door, but one I always manage to leave open a crack.

He's suddenly behind me, grabbing my hips and pushing me gently across the ice. He takes a knee, gliding and bringing me down with him. My butt now rests on his knee, and I lift my skates, laughing, flat-out cackling as he gives me a ride. When he rises and sets me back on the ice, I skate ahead of him, dying to try a scratch spin—a lightning-fast-in-place turn with crossed ankles and arms folded against your chest.

I set up for the turn, spotting Axel keeping his distance but watching me. Using weight distribution, I plunge into the spin, going faster and faster, the world turning into chaos around me. Did I mention it's been nearly twenty years since I've done any of this? As familiar as it all had felt, I forgot how to keep from getting dizzy. When I come out of the turn, I lose my balance and stupidly lean back. My skates start skidding underneath and away from me. I regain my composure, toppling forward, tripping, and—Axel catches me.

I'm at his mercy, my weight held by his arms, I stare up at him dumbly, not bothering to move yet. His hands feel strong at my back, despite this stupid pea coat, which is often too thin in colder temperatures, but now feels as thick as an iceberg.

Axel searches my face and grips me tighter to pull me upright. "I know you said you could take care of yourself, but I wouldn't have heard the end of it if I let you fall and you chipped a tooth or something on the ice." A masculine chuckle echoes from the pit of his stomach, and I'm so close to his chest, I can feel the rumble on my cheeks.

"Mmhm," I think I say, but I'm far too caught up in staring at Axel's lips. They're just plump enough to remain masculine and surrounded by his beard. Would the hair tickle? Would it make my mouth red?

My hands work their way up his exposed arms, the light scattering of blonde hair tantalizing my fingertips. Veins snake underneath his skin on the underside, and without thinking, without processing what I'm doing, I lean forward. Axel's gaze darkens once he realizes where this is going, and his hands press tighter to my back, pulling me closer to him. Our faces draw nearer, lips so close I can feel his breath against my skin—warm and minty.

"Heads up," a man's voice shouts, deep with a Chicagoan accent.

We jolt to attention, the voice belonging to a man on a Zamboni already driving around the rink to rewet the ice in time for hockey practice.

I clear my throat and reluctantly pull from Axel's grasp. "Guess we should get our notepads ready, hm?"

"Yeah," he starts, face stony, a wrinkle forming in his brow. "Guess we should."

Isn't this just like us? We almost have a moment—a tremendous one that would change the course of our relationship—and we pretend as if nothing happened. I wonder if his reasons are the same as mine. If I admit it, it boils down to one simple word: *fear*. And not fear of rejection or the unknown, but more so the trepidation that this would end like every other relationship I've had—heartbreak, disappointment, and a complete waste of time.

"Come on, Romance," Axel whispers, taking my hand and pulling me across the ice. "We don't need you getting run over by a damn Zamboni."

I stifle a laugh and let him pull me versus skating myself. When we're back on less slippery ground, I slip the guards over the blades and sit to undo the laces.

"How long has it been since you've skated?" Axel sat next to me, working the laces of his skates.

"Probably twenty years."

Axel's eyes go wide. "Wow. You looked great out there. Came right back to you, huh?" He leans one arm onto his knee, tightening the muscles and showing me just how *cut* he is.

"Yeah." I look away, feeling my cheeks warm, and let out a nervous laugh. "Except for that last spin, of course."

"Hey," Axel says gruffly.

Oh boy. Here we go.

"I hope I didn't make you uncomfortable." He wraps his knuckles against his thigh.

"Uncomfortable?" I slide the skates out of the way and dig my notepad from my purse.

Axel coughs into his fist and points at the ice. "Yeah. All the close quarters during that skate and everything."

The skating. *Zero* mentions of how close we were to swapping spit.

"Oh, *pfft*. No. Not at all." I sweep my hand through each pocket of my purse, unzip every zippered compartment, and can't find a single pen. "Platonic partners skate like that all the time together. That's all that was."

But I didn't want it to be. Is that what *he* wants?

Axel's fingers comb his beard, and he nods, his attention shifting to the hockey players entering the ice. "Yeah. Alright. Good." He slips a notepad no bigger than his hand from his back pants pocket and produces two pens, handing me one.

Biting my lower lip, I take it from him and whisper with the petiteness of a snowflake, "Thank you."

We sit in utter silence for all of practice, occasionally jotting notes and stealing glances at each other. We don't shy away from the proximity of seats so close together, but we don't bring up the almost-kiss. It's been brushed under the proverbial rug to be stomped on by everyone passing by. But the fleeting moment, the closeness, the skating, all of it is not nearly as confusing as the awareness of sitting in silence next to a man for an entire hour and not once feeling jittery or anxious.

EIGHT

AXEL

WHO WOULD'VE THOUGHT one could possess such an immense hatred for an inanimate object? That damn Zamboni. To say I'd been surprised seeing Theo arrive early to the rink *and* in skates would be grossly understated. And the shock I felt when she not only already knew how to skate but *that* well? The sight alone, I swear, got me semi rock hard. And I entirely blame that particular appendage for suggesting the duet skating because it wasn't a desire but a *need* to get my hands on her in any way I could.

But I didn't predict her stumbling and landing in my outstretched arms. Didn't anticipate the hammer my heart would become, pounding at my ribcage. Every neuron in my body told me to kiss her, but I didn't want to step over any unknown bounds. But then her gaze darting between my eyes and lips created this sort of hope she had the same thoughts. And we stood there too long, spent *way* too much time rationalizing the spark between us. If we'd have acted on impulse, we would've been halfway through the kiss by the time the Zamboni driver yelled at us.

I sit in my office chair, pausing after writing for another ten minutes because surely, I've punched out over four hundred words by now, right? Uh-huh. Try seventy-three. And it's been like this all day. I'll be lucky to have a whole page done of this article and sincerely hope the big Hawks game itself entices inspiration for both of us, or we're going to be up to our ears in Simone's wrath.

Life is currently being squeezed out of my R2-D2 stress ball. *Squeeze.* And why did Theo pretend as if we weren't about to kiss? *Squeeze—double squeeze.* Well, you *feiging*, you didn't exactly bring it up either, did you? And you *know* the reason for it happened years ago and you're still not over it.

Squeeeeeeze. And I don't stop squeezing until my hand shakes, elbow vibrating against my desk, and Mary passes with a nervous smile, trying to disguise her quickening pace.

"Someone's certainly tense." Rupert breezes from nowhere to the side of my desk and adjusts his purple bow tie.

With a disgruntled sigh, I rest the ball in its corner and rub my eye sockets furiously with the heels of my hands. "It's this damn article. I've never had writer's block like this. Ever."

"Want to know what I do when I need the creativity boost?" Rupert picks lint from his pants, flicking it over his shoulder.

I grab a pen and start clicking it. "I don't know. Is it—workplace appropriate?"

"Axel," Rupert yelps, gasping and holding back a smile. "I mean, yes, that could do wonders for just about anyone, but I personally take a walk. Specifically along Lake Shore Drive. You'd be surprised what the views in this city can do for the soul."

Rupert isn't wrong. The massive Lake Michigan extends past the horizon like an ocean, the Chicago River carving straight through the buildings, Navy Pier, and its giant Ferris wheel. And not to mention the architecture of the buildings and museums.

"You're right. That sounds nice, but—"

"Of course, I'm right," Rupert interrupts, tapping one stem on his glasses.

I let a chuckle push past my lips. "But—" I continue. "This thing isn't going to write itself, and we are going to the hockey game tonight."

Rupert's eye-roll could start a tidal wave. "Tonight. As in *hours* from now?"

Theo returns to her desk, having been away for an hour and twenty-two minutes. Not as if I took that much care to notice.

"Or maybe—" Rupert's face appears in front of mine, blocking my view of Theo. "This isn't about work at all."

"What are you talking about?" A gruffness overtakes my tone, and I rest my fingers on the keyboard, absently typing drivel, which I'll undoubtedly delete later.

Rupert leaps from my desk, one arm folding over his chest, the opposite elbow resting atop it. "Are you and Theo—" He pauses, snapping his attention to Theo, who steals a glance at me and redirects her gaze. "Oh, my stars, what is happening between you two?" Rupert turns back to face me, playfully swatting my desk.

"Nothing's happening. We're two writers assigned to work together for a sporty holiday romance story." I wince at what I typed: **Sports are fun and good, and yeah.** "Obviously, Simone is losing her edge with this harebrained idea."

"Excuse me?" Simone's commanding voice booms behind me, and if I hadn't gone to the restroom minutes earlier, I may have pissed my pants.

"She's behind me, isn't she?" Pitifully, I look to Rupert to throw me a lifesaver.

Rupert purses his lips and ominously nods while also retreating.

Great. Whatever happened to solidarity?

"Simone," I start, rising to my feet in complete preparation to eat my words from a damn trough if necessary. "I said that out of frustration and certainly didn't mean it."

"Frustration?" Simone lets her phone fall into a front jacket pocket and crosses her arms. "With what?" Her gaze takes on a new harshness.

She isn't buying my plea.

Do I admit that despite the words on my screen, none of them are worth a damn?

"Alright, I'll admit it wasn't a *complete* lie, but—" I press my fingertips into the grounding hard desk surface.

"That's better. I have zero respect for liars." Simone pulls her phone out, and her attention is back on its screen. "Something unclear about the assignment? Should I explain it in more layman's terms for you?"

Yowch.

"I mean no disrespect, ma'am, but I guess I'm trying to figure out what you hope to gain from our partnership. As it stands, I'm struggling to write a hockey column, a sport I'm very familiar with, because it needs to have *romance* and *holiday vibes* as well."

Simone laughs. Not just a light chuckle, but a "from the pit of your stomach rattles the light fixtures decibel-level" cackle. Heads turn in our direction, silent but staring, from everyone within earshot. This includes Theo, who leans back in her chair with widened eyes.

"Sorry. Did I miss something?" I ask, still pressing my hand against the desk *and* tapping my finger.

The giggles subside, Simone dabs tears from the corner of her eyes and pats my cheek like the sweetest of summer children. "Oh, Sports. You've both completely missed the point. You're supposed to be writing a story *together*. Make the sports side authentic enough to be published on NHL's website." She points her phone at me. "And as far as the romance? She writes it, sure, but you're telling me you've never been in a relationship?"

"I—" I am rendered speechless.

Simone wants us to co-author a piece? I've never done it, let alone in a genre I'm unfamiliar with and with a woman I'm *interested* in now.

"Sounds like you two have a lot of work to do after the game to meet your deadline. I suggest you figure out a new approach." Simone snaps her gaze to Theo, who jolts in her chair and slaps her hands on her keyboard. "Because this whole dazedly staring at your screens all day routine like lost puppies? It ends *today*."

And just like that, Simone hands me my own balls in a burlap sack.

I stand motionless, waiting for Simone to leave, but she snaps her fingers. "I meant now, Sports."

"Yes, ma'am." Clearing my throat, I snatch a notebook and pen.

Theo's hands grip her chair's armrests, eyes unblinking and borderline terrified. "What the hell happened over there?"

There's no reason I can't have a little fun with this, right?

"Listen. We're supposed to be working on this together, and as far as I can tell, all I have is a few bumbling sentences on hockey, and you—" I lean past her, reveling in the way her knees press together beneath her desk the closer I get. "—have written nothing?"

She taps her pen in a familiar staccato. *Carol of the Bells*, maybe? "It's a new Word doc. I wasn't feeling the previous draft."

"Oh, yeah?" I press a hip to her desk, still close enough to notice the light pink flushing her cheeks. "How did it start?"

"The—" Her jade eyes pin me, her teeth idly nibbling her bottom lip. "The ice rink."

An ice rink. The exact location of our "almost kiss."

"Do they go together, or did one show up after the other?" I open the notepad, pretending to jot scribbles.

She turns her chair to face me, the pen sliding through two

fingers as she flips it from point to end. "The heroine is surprised to find the hero already there—skating."

Electricity fizzles in the air between us, and I slide closer, shifting a knee to rest on the desk. Theo's throat bobs, and the pen flipping speed increases.

"Why is she surprised?" I ask, drawing stick figures on the blank page.

"She's yet to learn much about him. And is *pleasantly* surprised it's an interest they share."

My heart thunders in my chest. "And does she *want* to know more about him?"

"At this point in the story, it's the 'could this work?' beat." She stands and joins me, sitting on the desk.

"So, she's past the denial stage?" I swirl my pen on the paper, using the pattern to keep my sanity in check.

Theo nods, her gaze falling to my beard before making a lazy trail back to my eyes. "But she's questioning things. Guarding this." She traces a single finger over her left breast, and I'm fully aware she's referencing her heart, but I can't help staring at her porcelain skin.

How smooth is it to the touch? Did it flush pink like her neck and cheeks when aroused? How would her breasts feel cupped by my hands? In my mouth?

And when my salacious thoughts cause semi-wood to form in my pants, I push from the desk, acting aloof. "And what happens next in your story?"

"They skate, they laugh. She trips, but he catches her." Theo shifts on the desk, resting her hands in her lap as if she doesn't know what else to do with them. "And then—"

Theo entices my gaze, and such radiance glints in her eyes it makes my stomach tighten at the sight of it. "They almost—" I slide forward until our knees touch.

"They almost—" Her slender fingers are brushing my pants. "Kiss," she whispers.

"Aren't you two supposed to be at a hockey game?" Simone's voice booms like a thunderclap from her office. "Puck drop is in an hour."

I'm actually thankful for the interruption this time. I am. Because I'd been seconds away from kissing her in the *office*. Talk about bad ideas.

"Let me, uh—" Theo slips past me where I still stand numbly and out of sorts from what the hell just happened between us. "Let me grab my coat."

"Sounds good." I force the words out, but they fall from my lips raspy and my tone drops an octave. "I'll meet you by the door."

I catch Rupert and Desiree eavesdropping, their spines zipping straight when I glance at them. Desiree waves, a mischievous one with wiggling fingers. Rupert pantomimes two walking fingers and peers at me over the rim of his glasses.

Well, if Theo had no interest in *us*, these two certainly did.

Theo appears at my side, a messenger bag slung over her pea coat. She's already wearing her hat, gloves, and scarf, and pats the bag with a bright smile. "All set? I packed a few extra pens just in case and an extra notebook if things get really crazy."

"Plan on taking that many notes?" I grin at the adorable way she does a hitch step toward the door, beating me to hold it open for *me*.

She gestures for me to walk through like a snazzy hotel doorman. I oblige her, genuinely curious how long she'll remain mum about admitting we *did* almost kiss. But, it's far more entertaining this way. I can only hope that my silence over it too will have her insides in a twisted knotty mess.

"You never know, Ax. You never know," she answers, and we move to the elevators.

We make it to the train station and to the Hawks stadium, only engaging in small talk. The weather is surprisingly colder than previous years but hasn't snowed as much as we'd like. Auto gas prices have sky-rocketed, and we're thankful we don't own cars. At one point, she gets so desperate for conversation to avoid the gigantic elephant on the train that she asks about my favorite color, food, and animal—royal blue, pickled herring, and polar bear. I then have to explain what makes a herring pickled. She doesn't shy away from my proximity and only avoids eye contact once.

And as we walk into the arena after securing our press passes, it begs two questions: When do I do this? And how?

She heads to the restroom, and I buy us a tub of popcorn to share, remembering how much she indulged in the white cheddar powder they douse it in. Her smile when she returns is glorious and broadens when her gaze falls on the popcorn tub in my hand.

"You read my mind." Theo dances on the balls of her feet as she plucks several pieces in her mouth.

If only I had that ability.

It's difficult not to watch this woman eating, even if it is only popcorn. White residue from the cheddar power gathers on her bottom lip, and she licks it away, using the tip of her thumb to ensure there are no remnants in the corners. The center of her cheeks dimple as she chews, and she keeps the dirty hand raised like a surgeon. It's adorable and sexy as hell all at once.

We make our way to the seats, and she gasps at how close to the glass we are—directly behind and to the left of the Hawks bench.

"Well, we'll certainly be able to observe this close to the action," I mumble and plop into my seat, grimacing once my hip bumps the armrest.

Theo sits but swivels, her eyes beaming at the seas of people in bright red and white jerseys surrounding us. "Wow. This is triple the size of the crowd from the last game."

"Welcome to the big leagues, Romance." Grinning, I toss popcorn in my mouth.

The announcers ask everyone to rise for the national anthem— both the *Star-Spangled Banner* and *O Canada* given Chicago plays against a Canadian team. We stand with our hands over our chests, Theo tearing up when the giant American flag passes over the hands of hundreds of hockey fans in the seats on the other side of the ice. We clap when the singer ends with the word "brave," and Theo wipes the remaining tears from her eyes.

The first period soon begins, and Theo is on the edge of her seat, eyes following the puck's every move. Occasionally, she moves her gaze to the fans instead, pausing particularly on couples within the crowd and taking notes.

She leans closer to me, igniting my skin, and points to the box seats positioned up high and behind the goals. "Are those VIP seats or something?"

"They're more expensive, sure. And some of those people might be the players' families. Going to be hard to see them this far away, though."

Theo pulls the messenger bag to her lap and opens it with a flourish. "Good thing I came prepared." She pulls out a pair of binoculars and grins.

"Well played." I bump her arm with an elbow.

She raises the binoculars but pauses at this sudden and brief contact. The buzzing timer blares through the stadium, signifying the end of the first period, and neither team has scored a goal yet.

Unsurprisingly, the team mascot, a hawk, bustles through the stadium seating, entertaining everyone waiting by tossing t-shirts and dancing. When the song *Kiss Me* by Sixpence None the Richer starts blaring over the loudspeakers however, I'm frozen to my seat like a tongue to a metal pole in the dead of winter. The words

"Kiss Cam" blaze on the jumbotron, an older couple with silvering hair staring oblivious, appearing first. They jump in their seats and quickly peck each other on the lips.

The next couple is younger, college-age and their cheeks turn beet red. The woman vigorously shakes her head, holds up her beer, and kisses the plastic cup before chugging it down and smiling. But who they show next on the jumbotron has my insides melting into my shoes. Me. And. Theo.

The binoculars fall from her grasp, landing in a plastic clatter on the concrete floor. Everyone around us is cheering, whooping, and yelling for us to kiss. I turn in my seat, gauging her reaction, and she's already halfway toward me, giving me the same fluttering gaze as before—darting between my mouth and eyes, lips, and beard.

This is my chance.

Do or die, Nord.

Slipping my hand behind her neck, I lower my lips to hers and pause, her sweet and piney scent intoxicating my every thought. The roars of applause die from my ears as I press my lips to her supple ones. And I have full intention of ending it here—a quick peck to satisfy the cameras and the crowd, and get us past this awkward stage.

But Theo's hand is at the back of my head, her fingers bunching in my hair, and her lips move against mine. She tastes like popcorn and honey—a sweet and salty kiss that continues well after the camera has gone to the next couple. When she pulls away, a part of my very being escapes with her. An unease wracks my brain, fearing she'll think this is a mistake. She's clearly been hurt in the past if she found the need to tell me, even if it were in our playful story form, she's been protecting her heart. The tip of her middle finger drags over her bottom lip, and she stares at me.

"You okay?" I don't know what else to ask, what else to *say*.

She traces her thumb over the hair above my lip, gracing me with a half-smile. "Yeah."

The answer, her tone, isn't as optimistic and reassuring as I would've liked.

"Why don't you two get a room?" A man sitting behind us shouts, chuckling and raising his plastic cup of beer above his head when the crowd around us agrees.

Theo's cheeks blush crimson, and she sinks in her chair, laughing. I reach for her hand, testing if she'll let me take it. To my relief, she does, and I interlace our fingers. The second period begins, and that kiss clouds my brain so profusely I don't know what's going on in the game. Despite the ice and coolness hanging in the air, I'm positively on fire. I can't let it be our true first kiss. I'm better than that. She deserves to be wooed and not in front of thousands of people chanting at us.

"It's gotten unbelievably hot in here. Want to go for a walk?" I whisper against her ear.

A breath pushes from her lungs, and she squeezes my hand. "I hoped you'd ask something like that."

And I know the exact spot to take her. *Takk*, Rupert.

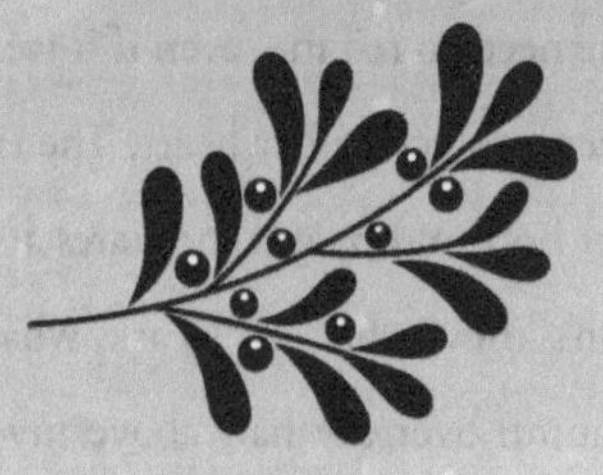

NINE

THEODORA

I AM PUTTY. I am goo. I'm all things that are boneless, mindless, and unable to speak because of Axel Nord and what's transpired between us the past twenty-four hours. We almost kissed. Then, we *did* kiss. Now, we walk along Lake Michigan side by side. And despite the temperature being in the frigid single digits, my skin blazes.

"I have to say, I've been to over a dozen hockey games in my time, and not once have I been on the Kiss Cam," Axel says, fully addressing what's been on both our minds since it happened.

I appreciate this.

"Oh, yeah?" Turning to walk backward, I tug his jacket sleeve at the elbow. "Taken a lot of women to these games?"

Axel's hands are in his pockets, but he slides them out and one-eye squints at me. "What the hell kind of loaded question is *that*,

Romance?"

He's right. It is.

"It wouldn't surprise me one bit." I stop walking, and he doesn't pause until we're standing with our toes touching. "You've got this roguish Scandinavian Viking deal going on. Blonde. Fiercely blue-eyed. And how long have you had that beard?"

The corners of his lips edge upward, and he rakes his finger through his beard. "For as long as I could manage to grow one. It wasn't this Viking-like in my twenties, though." A rumbly masculine chuckle escapes his chest. "But that's one of the many great things about writing for a career. They tend to not give a damn about the beard or tattoos."

The tattoo. Gravel coats my throat, my insides swooping. I can't keep my gaze from lingering over the arm with the full sleeve inked on it.

"Theo," Axel whispers, his bare hand finding my glove-covered one, loosely interlacing our fingers.

My heart becomes eight pairs of reindeer hooves pounding the ground. "Yes, Ax?"

"Come here." Slowly, he pulls me closer until our coats brush.

For the city, it's relatively quiet around us—the occasional blaring horn from traffic on Lake Shore Drive, the lake waves beating against the sand, the sporadic dedicated runner's feet striking pavement on the path behind us, and the faint melody of Frank Sinatra singing *The Christmas Song* from streetlight loudspeakers.

"I don't want that to be our first kiss. With you feeling pressured and thousands of people watching us." Axel removes one of my gloves, one tantalizing finger at a time.

Our. First. Kiss.

"Nothing pressured me. I was—" I cast my gaze downward, ashamed. "—scared."

Axel presses a single knuckle under my chin, and I swear to the universe it sends a sizzle through my jawbone. He coaxes me to look at him. "Why?"

"I've been hurt in the past. Badly, Axel."

Despite this gorgeous hunk of Norwegian man in front of me. Regardless of how much I want what I know is about to happen, it's enough to have tears forming in my eyes.

"Hey, now." He wipes the tears away, one, then the other. "I've been hurt too. My last ex not only cheated on me but stole thousands of dollars from me when I broke it off with her. But—"

Whoever this woman is, I hate her already. Cheaters are the absolute scum of the galaxy, and to *steal* on top of it? She must be Ursula in the flesh, and I secretly hope she has tentacles like her too.

"Axel, that is awful. No one should treat *anyone* like that." I squeeze his arm with my free hand.

Axel takes that hand, somehow managing an inviting smile despite the topic of conversation, and holds it. "*But* what's love if not risking fear every once in a while? It doesn't seem like it'd be as special to me."

My heart becomes the nut about to be cracked by the wooden soldier, and I *let* it.

"Are you sure you're not a romance writer?" I bite back a grin and edge closer to him, gulping at the hardness I feel pressing against my stomach. Heat pools in my stomach when he doesn't shy away from it, only pressing further into me.

His giant hands lift to my face, thumbs barely tracing my cheekbones. The rough calluses against my skin have my toes curling in my boots. Axel's gaze locks with mine, but it drops to my lips for a breath as if giving me an unspoken cue about what he intends to do.

For the love of anything holy, I need him to just *do* it.

His eyes lock back to mine, and he tilts his head to one side, a cocky grin pulling at the corner of his mouth as I'm already parting my lips. He's blissfully torturing me and knows it. His bottom lip brushes my top, a feather-like touch that leaves a whispered feeling behind. He pulls back only far enough so our mouths don't touch, but the closeness has our hot breath turning smoky from the cold, curling together in sensual tendrils.

Snow flurries begin to fall in glittering cascades around us, collecting in our hair and coats. The surrounding holiday lights make each flake pearlescent, casting shades of blue, purple, and pink fluttering like tiny, descending star beams. Axel moves one hand to my nape, his thumb trailing my collarbone, and then he bends forward and *kisses* me.

This is nothing like the stadium kiss. This is private and magical and so utterly perfect I want to squeal. But I don't. I can save the girly shrieks of delight for when I'm back in the safety of my apartment—alone.

His beard tickles my chin, but not enough to make me giggle. Instead, it sparks agonizing curiosity about how this beard would feel *elsewhere*. The thought has me whimpering into his mouth, my arms wrapping his neck. I rise on the balls of my feet, eager to bring us closer from our near colossal height difference. His tongue skirts the seam between my lips, and I open my mouth to him, our tongues twining together in a rhythmic dance. He leans forward, using his weight to guide me back to my feet, and bends to me, canting his head from left to right, taking the kiss deeper, more feral.

Axel moves a hand to the back of my head, fingers bunching my hair. His other arm encircles my waist, and he curves me backward, almost to the point of dipping me. Lazily, reluctantly, we pull away and stare at each other with hooded lids. Snowflakes have collected on my eyelashes, giving him a shimmering halo until I blink them away. And I know it's trope-y and cliché, but I swear I really do let out a breath I didn't realize I'd been holding the entire freaking *time*.

He pinches my chin with three fingers and wiggles it, grinning. "Better than the Kiss Cam?"

Is he kidding? This has thrown my entire outlook on *life* off its axis.

"What do you think?" With a pluckiness I didn't know I possessed, I slide my thigh up his hips, my non-gloved hand kneading the back of his neck.

A gravelly moan bubbles in the back of his throat, and his hand moves under my knee, hiking my leg further. "As much as I would love to continue this, we're still in the middle of a walking path in downtown Chicago, in below-freezing temperatures, and we should probably try and at least catch the last period of the game."

Being in one's right mind blows.

"Fine. Fine. You're right. Between that blonde hair and the snow you're starting to look like Santa Claus anyway." I laugh and brush the snow from his beard.

Smiling, he glares at me and shoves his beard in my face, swiping wetness over my cheeks. I shriek and wildly wave my hands at him.

"Could you do me one quick favor, though?" I ask, chewing on my bottom lip.

He's jostling more flakes from his beard and sneaks a quick peck on my forehead. "Anything."

"Would you—" I pause, making a steeple with my fingers and turning my hands upside down to reveal the "people" inside. "—pick me up and do a few twirls? I've always thought of this cute and beautiful scene in the snow where—"

Before I can finish, he's holding me with one arm under my knees, the other supporting my back. I yelp in delight, wrapping one of my arms around his neck, the other raising to the skies to catch snowflakes in my palm. The next instance, he has us turning so many circles the world blurs around me, and I let out the snorting cackle I do when inexplicably, uncontrollably, and deliriously happy.

We get back in time to see the last fifteen minutes of the game, and I manage to take several notes on observing how supportive some of the players' wives are compared to others. Some look as if they'd prefer to be anywhere else other than a hockey game, and I intend to ask them as many questions as the happier ones. Axel gets access to the press area of the locker room to interview players while I head straight for the green room, where the families wait for their guys.

I catch myself smiling like a fool as I make my way through the hallway, the feel of his beard tickling my lips and chin still very much there like a phantom touch. And the ever-rising heat between us both sexually and physically, combined with the cool wetness from descending snow, made a surreal mix of icy hot I wasn't sure I ever wanted to let go of.

With my press badge hanging visibly from a lanyard around my neck, I push through the green room doors to dozens of women and children chattering at tables. A table of various snacks, including cheese, crackers, holiday cookies, bags of chips, and fruit, rests in the corner. Another side table has bottled water, sodas, and select alcoholic beverages. I grab a water, scanning the women and studying them before deciding on asking one for an interview.

A beautiful brunette sits with two children who both under ten, running circles around her. She sighs, hanging her head in her hand. "I told you all a dozen times, do not run. Please."

Chewing my lip, I approach her and extend my hand. The sudden stranger appearing from nowhere has the kids stopping shyly, crowding around their mom. "Hi there. My name's Theodora Hackett, and I'm a column writer for Celestial Magazine."

"Wow. I'm used to hearing Sports Weekly or one of the local newspapers. Not a contemporary magazine." The woman shakes my hand, her kids gradually inching out from behind her. "My name's Ramona Malone."

"Pleasure to meet you, Ramona. I'm working on a holiday short story romance revolving around hockey. Would you mind if I ask you a few questions?" I motion to the seat across from her.

"Romance? In hockey?" She snorts and nods at the seat.

I sit and rest my bag on the table. One child reaches for it, and the mother snatches his wrist, frowning and wagging a finger. "Well, how did you and your husband meet?"

"College." Ramona smiles as she stares absently at the table as if playing out the moment in her head.

An idea immediately sparks—a second chance romance for former college flings. Let's call them Amanda and Kyle for now. They're brought together again by hockey when Amanda attends a game with a date. The only reason they'd separated was Amanda's move to another state to get her master's and eventual doctorate degree while Kyle was drafted to the NHL and moved to Canada. They haven't seen each other since.

"I'd love to know details if you're willing?" Offering her a friendly smile, I let the tip of my pen rest on the notepad.

"Oh, sure. I'm just not used to these kinds of questions. It's refreshing, honestly." Ramona adjusts in her seat and crosses her legs. "I was a cheerleader."

I tilt my head to one side like a dog trying to make sense of a silly human word. "There are cheerleaders in hockey?"

She chuckles at this, her eyes lighting up. "No. I mean not exactly, not in the sense you're familiar with."

I suspect she's not used to this sort of attention because her husband is typically the one interviewers surround for questioning.

"I was a basketball cheerleader."

"Wow. Now I'm even more curious about how you two met. In a class, maybe?" I doodle hearts of varying sizes in the margins of my legal pad.

"Nope. He was a year above me and a different major, so none of our classes overlapped." Her cheeks turn red, and she lets her face fall in her hand, laughing. "We met in a men's locker room."

I gasp, over-exaggerating it. "Nuh-uh."

"Yup. It was my first year, and I didn't know my way around." Ramona chews her thumbnail. "Thank God Charlie was the only one in there."

This makes me pause, thinking about me and Axel's "meet cute"—the elevator incident, a mysterious new project forcing us into proximity, and the deliberate mistaken identity performed by yours truly. It'd make for quite a fun story to tell grandkids, that's for sure.

"And were you two together ever since then?" I'm now filling the hearts in with black ink.

"Yes. College sweethearts. He proposed to me before being drafted. I had one more year, and we had another thing keeping us tied together." She ruffles one of the kids' heads, a boy with a mop of black hair and glasses. "I was pregnant with Charlie, Jr. here."

"Ew, Mom," Charlie whines, batting her hand away.

Smiling, I debate my next words carefully. "I imagine the perks of being a hockey family are obvious to most. But what specifically do you find the hardest?"

Ramona sighs after securing the glasses on Charlie's nose that are sliding off. "How often he's not home for weeks or months can be tough. But holidays are especially troublesome."

I add more to my growing idea for a story: Kyle schemes an elaborate holiday surprise at the rink that includes ice skating. "Do they schedule games on holidays?"

"No. The NHL is good about giving Thanksgiving, Christmas Eve, and Christmas day off. But it's as if he breezes in and whisks right back out." Ramona frowns, looking at her children. "If it were just me, I could deal with it, but watching their disappointment, that's what makes it difficult."

"I get that. But it could be worse?" I one-shoulder shrug when she snaps her gaze to me. "You could be a football wife? They have games on Thanksgiving *and* Christmas day."

Her eyes do a sort of fluttery blink at this revelation. "I've never thought about that. You're right."

"Has your husband ever done a grand gesture around the holidays?"

I can't help myself.

"Oh, yes. He's dressed up as Santa more times than I can count. Surprised me once during a hockey game right before Christmas Eve by doing the giant poster board message deal from *Love Actually* behind the glass in full hockey uniform in between periods. And he's baked cookies and wrapped presents with the kids while I had a spa day." Ramona's eyes glisten. "Last year, he bought this Disney Funko Pop Advent Calendar. I thought it was for the kids, but he got it for me. I *love* Disney."

After jotting all of this down and then some, I extend my hand with a grin. "This was amazing. Thank you so much for sharing with me."

"I hope you find it useful, and I can't wait to read it."

An hour goes by and I've interviewed several more of the wives. Most share the same sentiment as Ramona with their husband's time away from home, but each has such glowing things to say about things the players did when they were home. It's enough information and inspiration to write an entire novel, not just a short story column for a magazine.

When I exit the hallway, Axel is still in the locker room, and I find myself leaning against the wall, waiting for him. I *could* call an Uber, but given what happened between us, I don't want him to think I'm ditching him.

Instead, my writer's brain goes into overdrive, creating plot threads for a genre I've never written—historical fiction. And more specifically? The Viking Age.

A blonde Viking, clad in armor and wielding an ax. He takes off his helmet to reveal he looks—exactly like Axel. Having closed my eyes to let my imagination run wild, I blink them open confusedly. You know what? I'm rolling with it.

Grey storm clouds are in the sky, making Axel's blue eyes downright iridescent. I peek through the tent flaps.

I do? And now I'm the heroine in this story. Typical.

I spy him stalking toward the tent, taking off bits of armor as he goes, leaving it all in a scattered mess in his wake.

He ducks into the tent, and his lips meet mine in a fierce kiss. He smells like dirt, blood, and sweat. The idea of it caked on his hands and face, smearing my skin, should disgust me, but all it does is tighten my insides and make me more ravenous for him. He pulls away only long enough to shrug my linen dress from my shoulders, exposing my breasts. He kneads, licks, sucks, and nips them before wrapping his hands around my hips.

In one swift motion, he effortlessly lifts me from the ground. He moves us to the other side of the tent, resting me atop the table. He sweeps his arm across the items strewn on it, sending wooden bowls, apples, and a half-eaten chunk of bread clamoring to the floor. He whips the linen shirt from his torso, revealing a bronzed muscular chest and stomach. The full sleeve tattoo courses up his arm, over the shoulder, and a part continues onto one pec. His hand is on his belt, quickly undoing it and freeing his hardness for me. He bunches my dress' skirts at my waist and pulls me to the edge of the table by the backs of my knees. Without caution or warning, he plunges into me, deep and rough. He thrusts over and over and—

"What are you daydreaming about?" Axel's deep voice rumbles in my ear.

I snap my eyes open, not realizing I'd been fondling my neck. Please tell me he didn't stroll into the hallway to find me moaning, too.

"I uh—was going over the story idea I came up with from speaking to the wives."

Axel presses a forearm on the wall near my head, and I swear if he adds another, completing the "cage-in," I will have my way with him right here in the hallway. Public indecency be damned. "Must be some story. Heard you mumbling words that sounded a lot like 'armor' and 'thrust.'"

The way he says "thrust" in that Norwegian accent has a pool party developing in my panties.

"Mmhm," Axel says, one thousand percent calling my bull crap. "Busted, Romance."

"Okay, so it's a genre piece. A separate novel I'm considering writing." I press the back of my head against the sturdy wall behind me.

Axel's nose brushes mine before he pushes away, chuckling. "And whatever inspired *that* all of a sudden?" His tone is all forms of teasing and sarcasm.

"A desire to write beyond contemporary romance?" I manage a grin that feels like a grimace.

He lets out a breathy laugh and juts his elbow to the side, offering me his arm. "Ready to head home?"

Home. Like *his* home? Oh, crud. I'm not ready for this. I'm—completely blowing this out of proportion.

"My home? And you to *your* home?"

A rousing chuckle putters from his stomach now. "Yes, Theo. You're acting stranger than normal. Are you okay?" The back of his hand presses to my forehead, and I nuzzle it like an attention-deprived golden retriever. "Theo?"

My eyes burst open. "Yes?"

Axel leans down, pressing a chaste kiss to my lips, his hand moving from my head to my cheek. "Seriously. You alright?"

"Never better. Did you get everything you needed from the hockey players?"

Axel curls me to his side and kisses the top of my head. We walk with locked arms and share stories from the players and their wives. I tell him my *non*-salacious story idea about the two college sweethearts, and we continue to hit it off at every turn.

We're already working so well together on the article, we've kissed, and we can share silence together. Maybe there *is* the possibility of us being something more than two writing colleagues who occasionally like to make out. Maybe this really *could* work.

TEN

AXEL

I'VE BEEN INTERVIEWING several players for the past hour, managing to take a few notes because I *am* a professional, but to say I give them my undivided attention? Not even close. Feelings consume my every thought. Theo's lips—soft and thin. The way her body pressed into mine, exploring what I had to offer beneath layers of clothing. The moans and groans that escaped her throat when I swirled my tongue with hers.

"Hey, man."

My gaze snaps in Charlie Malone's direction—the hockey player I've been interviewing, and seemingly zoned out for the past thirty seconds. At least, I sure as hell hope it's been only thirty seconds.

"You, uh, alright?" Charlie points at my hand crumpling the top page of my notepad. He's missing a front tooth, and it stands out when he laughs.

Coughing into my fist, I smooth the page as best I can, wincing at the notes I managed to distort further from my usual chicken scratch. "Yeah. Sorry. Got a lot on my mind, you know? Holidays and all."

Charlie nods, a single wavy piece of dark hair falling over his gaze, still wet with sweat. "I get it, man." He scratches the days-worth collected stubble under his chin. "Can't wait for the last game of the season so I can surprise my family. Going all out this year."

"Oh, yeah?" I ready my pen. "Mind if I ask what your plan is?"

Charlie licks his lips and glances around us like his family is about to pop up out of nowhere in the locker room. He goes so far as to drape an arm over my shoulders and lead me to a corner away from the rest of his team. "Disney World."

Two little words, and no one ever has to elaborate.

"Wow, dude. Your kids are going to flip. How old are they?" I scribble "Disney vacation."

After jostling me, Charlie slaps his palms together. "Perfect ages. Six and nine. Plus? My wife is the biggest Disney freak you'd ever meet. She may even enjoy it more than our kids." Charlie chuckles, his face lighting up like a hearth's warm glow.

"That's awesome. Enjoy it."

The idea of being a husband to someone and, even more crazily, a *father* rattles my brain every few months. It's become more frequent once I hit the sweet age of thirty-five. Did men have one of those internal biological clock deals, too? Because it's like someone flipped a switch. And because seeing Charlie's proud expression and sheer selfless plan to make his family happy gave me a twinge of jealousy tells me my days of bar hopping have long been over.

I thank Charlie for answering all my questions, pause for a few photos, and head for the hallway to wait for Theo to finish. That is if she hasn't high-tailed it out of the building already from fear of having to face the aftermath of our life-changing kiss.

I'm expecting an empty hallway to greet me but couldn't have predicted the sight of Theo leaning against a wall with her fingers delicately tracing over her collarbones—one to the other, back and forth. Her eyes are closed, and if I didn't know any better, she was biting her lower lip. I should've cleared my throat, coughed, pretended to sneeze to alert her to my presence but I'm far too entranced to give a damn. Is she having the most vivid daydream I've ever witnessed? And if she is, please make the dream about *me* for the love of all the known cosmos.

When she lets out a sensual gasp, I cross the space between us. Despite no one being around, I don't want to risk *anyone* showing up out of the blue and witnessing her like *this*—so sultry and vulnerable.

After breathing in her fragrance, I lower my lips near her ear and whisper, "What are you daydreaming about?"

I don't expect her to admit it, and she doesn't disappoint by immediately derailing, contemplating no doubt how much of this I've seen. Her gaze keeps falling to my lips, especially when I speak, and it takes everything in me not to reenact our moment from Lake Shore Drive. My body eclipses hers. It'd be easy to cover her if someone walks by.

The nerves bubbling from her chest when I ask if she's ready to go home make a chuckle escape. And the fact she has to confirm by asking versus declaring she's *definitely* going to her own home sends a surge down my spine. She curls her arm with mine, and we head outside.

"I may have come up with a concept we could use for the story after talking with one of the players' wives," Theo chirps, bouncing on her heels in delight.

Damn, she's adorable *and* hot. How did she manage it?

"Well, let's hear it." I pull her closer to my side when I catch her shivering.

She leans the back of her head against my arm and uses the other hand to gesture at the sky. "Imagine this. A second chance romance. Former college lovers. She goes off to get her doctorate in another state. He gets drafted in the NHL and moves to Canada." With child-like wonder playing in her eyes, she nods gingerly at me. "With me so far?"

"You're on a roll, Romance."

"Good. Because this is the best part." Her gloved hand playfully swats my chest and she walks backward in front of me. "They never think they'll see each other again, go on with their lives, and a decade later? Whamm-o." She slaps her hands together.

I crack a smile and purposely slow my stride so as not to lap her tiny steps. "Serendipitous events?"

"Serendipitous? Wow. But yes. She goes to a game with a date, and guess who's on the enemy team?" Theo rubs her hands together and uses one palm to warm her nose afterward.

I comb my beard with two fingers, contemplating her unraveling plotline. "You may be onto something here. I know we said we were each heading home, but did you want to pop into the office? Maybe write some of this out while it's fresh in our minds?"

And give me an excuse disguised as work to spend as many waking moments with you as you'll give me?

She shrieks and hoists both fists in the air. "That's a brilliant idea, Axel. Let's hurry before I lose my mojo." Theo scurries past me.

Laughing and lightly hooking her arm, I stay put and coax her back to me. "You planning on taking the scenic route there?"

Her emerald eyes blink as she notices the lake in the direction she almost mistakenly took. "I really *am* excited about this."

"There's a lot to be excited for lately," I say, dropping my tone and turning her to face me. Bending, I press a light kiss at the corner of her lips.

"To quote one of my favorite Christmas movies, *Elf*—you missed." Theo positively beams at me, fingers plucking at her coat's hem.

Aside from the "Son of a Nutcracker" quote, all others escape me from that film. But it could also be most of my blood leaving my brain for regions further...down.

"What?" I ask with a chuckle, bumping a knuckle under her chin.

She taps a finger against the center of her lips. "You. Missed."

It's official. I'm an idiot.

Grinning, I press my lips to hers, *entirely* on hers, but try to turn it into a kiss. Instead, I trap her within my arms, and mouths still connected; I say from the corner of mine, "This better?" It comes out ridiculous and muffled but has her laughing hysterically.

Coyly, she pushes at my chest, still giggling. "My nose is stuffy, and I can't breathe," she squeals out, and after I peel away, she gives my cheek a tiny peck.

Moments later, we're back in the office. Everyone has long since gone home for the night, and the space is blissfully quiet. Darkness blankets every corner save for the tree lit up in the center, spilling multi-color bursts of warm light over our desks. I move for the light switches, ready to flick one on, but Theo's tender hand rests on my forearm, stopping me.

"I love it like this. It makes me feel calm and all gooey on the inside." Theo's smiling but staring at the tree versus looking at me.

I can think of a few other things that would make her feel similarly.

"It does paint a certain level of serenity. Quiet space that's normally bustling with activity and chatter." I take her hand, leading us to my desk. where I sit with spread legs, guiding her between them. "This lighting is a million times better than the gaudy headache-inducing fluorescents."

She rests her hands on my thighs, nodding and still stealing glances at the tree over my shoulder. "There's also a bit of nostalgia attached to it for me, I guess."

When I say nothing but quirk a brow, she continues.

"As a kid, before presents started taking up all the space on the tree skirt, I used to lie underneath it, staring up through the branches for way longer than should entertain a kid." A bittersweet laugh bumbles from her throat, and she squeezes my leg. "It's just so sparkly and glowing and a unique way to view it."

Moving to America with my family's traditions around the holidays held firmly in my heart made it difficult to connect with anyone else, *truly* click, when I couldn't make it home to Norway. There were few I'd even dare to confess to for fear of insulting someone or causing some misunderstanding. But for whatever reason, I feel comfortable around Theo. Like she wouldn't give a damn how I celebrated, she'd simply be elated that I enjoy this time of year as much as she did.

"What does Theo Hackett do normally around the holidays?" I slide my palms up her sides until my hands grip her hips. "Christmas Eve mass? Watch a Nativity scene play?"

"I did all that stuff when I was younger, sure."

I drum my fingers on her waist. "But not anymore?"

"This is going to sound awful but once I moved out of my parents' house and out on my own, started my writing career, we started seeing each other less and less. They were always afraid of bothering me or interrupting me and I became so consumed with work I'd honestly forget how long it'd been since I saw them."

"Children change. We're not supposed to be carbon copies of our parents. We're meant to become our *own* people." I graze the back of my hand over her cheek, frowning at the way her chin quivers with obvious guilt.

"But I'm an only child. I'm all they've got."

"They have each other too, Theo. That's why they said those vows."

She sniffles and shrugs. "True. Hence why once they retired, they started to go to Fiji every year for Christmas. Particularly, when I gave them my blessing because we can see each other and celebrate any time of the year. They deserve to enjoy themselves while they still can in whatever way makes them happy."

"There you go. Anyone who started this whole deal that you *must* see family on the holidays or you're some kind of bad person or something, is off the mark in my humblest opinion." I knead her skin through her shirt with the tips of my fingers. "For what? To be stressed and possibly argue and feel obligated to get everyone a gift? It's taking away what makes it special in the first place."

Theo's eyes light up and she bites the inside of her cheek, gaze casting to the floor instead of me or the tree. Her eyes pinch shut, and she lifts her hands to my shoulders, suddenly blowing out a breath. I am a six-year-old boy about to be told Santa Claus isn't real.

"I want to tell you something I've never told anyone else, but I'm terrified you'll take it wrong." Theo still doesn't look at me, her fingernails flicking the seam of my pants.

I scootch from the desk, basking in her bewildered expression as I take her hand and lead her toward the tree. "Let's go to your happy place first, then. Because I can promise you there are very few things, if any, you can tell me that I'd take offensively."

She's hesitant at first, but soon, she's nestled under the tree with her hands resting on her stomach. It takes a bit of maneuvering on my part, but I find a singular spot where my eyes aren't getting poked by fake tree branches and rest my head on my folded hands behind me.

"I absolutely love this time of year. The vibrance in the air, the smells, the togetherness, magic, and wonderment." Theo feels around for my hand, and I offer her one, interlacing our fingers. "But I've never felt connected to the—reason for the season."

A tightness ribbons in my chest.

"You mean the Christmas aspect of it all?" I grip her hand tighter.

She turns on her side, her face appearing within inches of mine. "Yes. I grew up with it all. Know the story. I never naïvely thought December twenty-fifth was Santa Claus's birthday versus Jesus, or anything, but at dinner, I'd say the prayers out of respect but never knew *why*."

Theodora Hackett is a woman plucked from another celestial plane and plopped in my path. There's no other explanation for it.

"In Norway, growing up, my family would celebrate a hybrid of traditions." I pull her close until her chin rests on my chest and her fingers play with my beard.

"Hybrid?"

Sweeping hair from her eyes, I nod. "We always have a Christmas tree. We even hang paper star lanterns and whatnot, but we start celebrating on the winter solstice. We call it *Jul* or Yule."

Theo perks up at this, moving to lean on her elbow and yelping when the tree defies her efforts. Sinking back to her shoulder, she nuzzles into me. "And you celebrate for more than a day or two?"

"Yes. Twelve days, to be specific. The whole idea behind it is celebrating the sun's rebirth because it's the shortest day of the year." I absently run my fingers through her hair, feeling the soft sleekness of fiery tendrils against my rough skin.

"Axel." My name pushes from her throat in a sultry moan, and if it wasn't for being partially trapped under a tree, I may have rolled on top of her.

"Yes?"

"Will you share more with me about *Jul*? About all the traditions? The history?" Theo's hand sneaks under my shirt, her frigid fingers against my stomach shocking at first.

The fact that she not only wants to know more about my culture's holiday traditions but also bothered to call it *Jul* has me ravenous for this woman. I want to know more about her background, family, future plans, hopes and dreams. And I want her physically, emotionally, and in every way possible—I feel like I've known her for a lifetime already.

"I'll tell you and show you *everything*." Curling to the side as much as the space allows, I cup her cheek and press my lips to hers, making swirling patterns against her skin with my thumb.

Theo's tongue curls with mine, the hand under my shirt exploring higher, a moan vibrating against my mouth from her as nails find my pecs. She bites my bottom lip, her hips pressing against mine, the hardness straining in my jeans pressing into her. Then she disappears, scooting from under the tree and urging me to do the same. I'm standing upright for three seconds before Theo leaps into my arms, trusting I'll catch her—and I do. We become a hurricane of nips, nibbles, moans, and licks as I walk to my desk and sit her there.

Theo pulls away with a wicked grin perking her lips, hands greedily reaching for my shirt to peek at what she'd been groping moments prior. Her smile fades, eyes becoming hooded, and she stares at my abs for what feels like an eternity. "Axel, are you even *real?*"

"And here I thought seeing is believing?" A throaty chuckle escapes me, and all I can do is stand there while the woman of my dreams ogles my muscles and pokes them, testing if they'd— deflate?

"Tell me another thing about *Jul*," Theo demands, leaning back on her elbows and giving me those come-hither eyes.

Groaning, I crawl over the top of her, unbuttoning only one of her shirt buttons, where I kiss the exposed skin of her stomach, teasing her. "We decorate with goats made of straw and red ribbon. And some versions of the stories say it stemmed from Thor's two goats."

Her head had been hanging back, moaning, but it pops up at

this, and she goes silent. "Thor?"

Moving further up, I trail kisses across her collarbones, scraping my beard over her already-flushed pink skin. "Uh-huh. Don't make me jealous of a Norse god now, Romance." I smile into the kiss I give her, and she grins back.

She stops asking questions and pours more into kissing me, fingers unabashedly climbing up my shirt again, roaming my back and shoulders. I massage one breast through her shirt and bra, feeling sixteen again in a heated make-out session somewhere I shouldn't be doing it. The thought should've made me stop, should've brought rational recollection back, but it only egged me further.

She pants into the kiss, her one hand grabbing my ass and groaning at the feel of it. A leg wraps around my waist, and she pulls me tighter to her, making me grunt as my junk gets smashed into the table.

Her eyes fly open with horror, every part of her frozen. "Oh, my—Axel, I'm so sorry. I forget how freaking tall you are."

Laughing and secretly thanking the stars above, it wasn't my balls that took most of the impact, I trace a thumb over her lips. "I'm fine. Life would be pretty boring if everything went perfectly all the time, right?"

A newfound determination glints in her eyes, and her hands bunch my shirt, using me to lift her and kissing me again.

That's until fluorescent lights spill around us, brightening the room in gaudy white. We both still, and a faint whistling of *Jingle Bells* has us fumbling to fix ourselves, to make it appear we weren't just about to screw on my desk in the middle of the night. Someone rounds the corner. The janitor. He nearly jumps out of his skin when he spots us. The mop he holds bounces to the floor, and he pushes a hand over his chest. He's middle-aged with dark hair turned white at the temples, and his thick mustache bristles when he sneers at us.

"You two about gave me a heart attack. Do you have any idea what time it is?" The janitor points between us.

I'm now in my office chair, typing on a keyboard on a black screen while Theo sits across from me with a pen in hand and no paper in sight. "I guess we lost track. When inspiration strikes, my friend. Am I right?"

Theo flashes me a mischievous grin and chews on the butt of the pen.

"I wouldn't know, but I'll take your word for it." The janitor shakes his head and supports himself on one knee to scoop the mop back in hand.

"We'll get out of your way. Sorry for startling you." Theo stands and motions for me to follow.

After grabbing our coats and briefcases, we meet in the atrium. Despite having kissed three times now, this one felt more intimate and has an unseen charge zipping between us.

"It's almost one in the morning. I should head home. We've got a lot of work to do tomorrow to give Simone something. She'll expect it. Not to mention Rupert wants me to help him pick out the wardrobe for his next photoshoot." Theo uses a single finger to fix a part of my beard that's become unkempt.

Adjusting my jacket for no reason other than I don't know what the hell else to do, I kiss her cheek. "You're right. We've got plenty of time to see where this goes."

At this, she surprises me with a brightened smile. "Yes. Yes, we do."

I've received plenty of *Jul* gifts in my lifetime, but if this works out with Theo, and every fiber in me is praying it does, this could be the most cherished of all.

ELEVEN

THEODORA

I'VE REVERTED TO a five-year-old version of myself pretending to sleep on Christmas Eve in unruly anticipation of what's to come. But instead of revolving around a portly man in a red suit with a snow-white beard, this centers on a burly Viking with eyes the color of Neptune. It's bad enough that I can't stop staring at him when we're in the same vicinity. And worse, my brain insists on replaying our heated office make-out session on loop. It's more inconvenient when helping a friend choose the wardrobe for an upcoming men's fashion photoshoot, as I am right now.

"Theodora," Rupert shouts, snapping his fingers in my face.

I sit on the bench outside the fitting rooms at some couture clothing shop I didn't bother remembering the name of. I'm resting my head on the partition behind me when Rupert has to jolt me to attention for the third time since we arrived. "Sorry. I didn't get a lot of sleep last night."

"Oh, yeah?" Rupert folds his arms. He's changed into a shiny black button-down, glossy skinny pants, and a red plaid jacket that falls to his knees. "This have anything to do with a six-foot-four Norwegian?"

Is he really that tall? That's like Dwayne "The Rock" Johnson tall.

I move my purse to my lap and zip up my spine. "I'm confused. Does what have to do with Axel? My lack of sleep or—"

"Ah ha!" Rupert points at me and waves that same finger in my face. "You *are* thinking about Axel."

Playfully batting his hand away, I push to my feet. "How many other tall Norwegian guys do we know?"

Rupert arches a brow and stares at his cuticles. "You'd be surprised."

My hands fly to my head, frustration brewing, but I fight everything in me not to take it out on innocent, popular with the boys, Rupert. "Okay, *me*. How many tall Norwegian guys do *I* know?"

"Sweetie." With one hand clasped to his chest, Rupert places the other on my shoulder and pouts. "I don't know your life."

Exasperatedly, I let out a tigress growl that comes out more like a cub. "Rupert, we're here to find clothes for your photoshoot. Not talk about Axel freaking Nord."

"Well, no offense." He places a fist on his hip. "But you're pretty useless when you keep zoning out every three minutes."

My mouth opens to object but no words that will successfully defend myself in this situation come out. I pinch the bridge of my nose. "Fine. Things have—escalated? Between me and Axel?"

Rupert lowers his glasses, giving me "you dirty little hoe" eyes before sliding them back in place. "This I have to hear."

"That outfit is banging, by the way. Make that one you use." I paint an imaginary line with my finger, fanning it up and down over Rupert's body.

"Fab." Rupert flicks the jacket collar. "Going to hop into the next one. Seven to go. But start talking. I'm sure I can manage to hear you through plywood." He wraps his knuckles against the fitting room door and whisks inside.

Where do I begin? Go all the way back to when we almost kissed while skating? No. Rupert will never let me live it down, knowing it's been days, and I never told him anything about it.

"So, we went to the hockey game, right?" I hug myself for comfort.

"Uh-huh, and they put you two on Kiss Cam," Rupert says from inside the fitting room, giggling.

My heart javelins from my chest to my toes. "How did you know that?" I spin on my heel, impatiently pacing, waiting for him to come out.

Rupert's casually leaning on the doorframe when it opens, his hips jutted to one side like the diva he is. He's now wearing black slick pants and a black long-sleeved shirt with a white exaggerated collar sticking out from beneath it. "Saw it on TV. Wondered how long it would take for you to spill the beans."

"You don't watch sports. And that outfit is a major no. You look like Wednesday Adams and not in a good way."

Rupert frowns and fiddles with the collar. "What if I added a pigtail wig?"

"No," I snarl, pointing at the fitting room.

He rolls his eyes and dramatically dives back in, closing the door with a flourish. "I was on a date, and it happened to be playing on one of the TVs. I hadn't been paying any attention, but when your two faces pop up on screen? Well, honey, it's hard to ignore."

Groaning, I flop back to the bench, hunching and letting my face fall in my hands.

How many other people I know saw it? The thought hadn't even crossed my mind at the time—*live* sports. Major league. Ugh it all.

"I think I'm going to be sick," I say into my hands.

Rupert gasps. "Are you pregnant?"

"What?" I slap my palms to my knees. "No. That'd involve, oh, I don't know, *coitus*?"

Rupert's nose twitches, and he gags on thin air. "Honestly, Theo, who calls it that?"

I make a puppet out of my hand and hold it between us, moving the "mouth" as I speak robotically. "We have not had sex. Only kissed." Pausing, I turn the puppet toward my face, sigh, and shrug, before spinning it back to face Rupert. "Several times."

Rupert holds up a hand, indicating I should stop talking. "Pause right there, sister. I need you to tell me this to my face, but I must try the rest of these outfits on." He sashays back into the dressing room, and I yelp when my phone vibrates in my pocket.

As I trace a finger over my lips, I realize Axel's mouth left an imprint against my skin. Every place he touched—I trail my fingers across my collarbones, stomach, and cheek. I don't want that feeling to go away. I want it *everywhere*—down to my damn elbow.

"Uh-huh," Rupert says all-knowingly. "If you don't admit you're bonkers for this guy, I may have to disown you, honey." He sports a black velvet jacket with gold foil filigree embroidered on the border, no shirt, and those same black skinny pants.

"That one is a keeper," I say this mostly because I don't want to admit anything to Rupert nor *think* about our kisses.

Rupert doesn't budge. "Great. The kisses explanation now, please."

There's no winning this one.

I rattle the words with the speed of an auctioneer. "Almost kiss skating. Kiss on Kiss Cam. Axel asks to go for a walk, says that wouldn't be our first kiss, and he kisses me again on Lake Shore Drive with the lights and the music, and it starts snowing, and it's almost too perfect for words. And he twirls me. Twirls. Me."

When I finally get the nerve to glance at Rupert, his eyes glisten and his bottom lip trembles.

"The big hulking brute is a romantic?" Rupert bites his knuckle.

He doesn't know the half of it. But the moment under the tree with Axel? That's one I'll reserve for me and me alone.

"He's seemingly this perfect mix between brawn, brains, and

bliss." A smile flutters over my lips, and I feel this sudden urge to see Axel. Even to say hi and see him grinning at me.

Rupert slides in front of me, unblinking and lips pulled into a thin line. "If you don't pursue him, Theodora, I swear, *I* will. Gay or not, I *will* try."

As joking as Rupert's words are, a surge of surprising possessiveness bubbles in my core. It's not like Axel is mine by any form of the word. Heck, he's not even my boyfriend. The realization makes my limbs numb.

"Would you be mad if I ditched you?" I display a frown to rival a circus clown.

"Not if it's to get your cute ass back to the office and make googly eyes at Axel." Rupert's shoulder bumps against mine.

After giving Rupert a quick peck on the cheek, I sprint out the door and make my way to the office.

Knowing Axel's desk will be directly to my left, the jitters that overcome me when I round the corner are uncontrollable. No, not jitters. Titillating goosebumps are more like it. And when his head lifts, as if sensing my presence, and that panty-dropping smile graces his mouth? I'm drowning in his sea-blue eyes and letting myself sink to the sandy bottom.

"Hey," I say, combing my hair over one ear, my feet turning toward themselves pigeon-toed style.

After tapping his pen against his desk twice, Axel rises and slides his hands into his pockets. "Hey. Aren't you supposed to be helping Rupert?"

"Yup." I lift my chin high and glide to my desk, throwing all my belongings on it, and draping my jacket over the chair.

That deep, gravelly chuckle of Axel's rumbles at my side. "Okay, so what are you doing here?"

"I couldn't keep focused. My mind was—elsewhere." Fully aware of what I'm doing, I bend over my desk, taking the mouse in hand and wiggling it to wake up the screen.

Not disappointing, Axel's gaze drops to my butt, sweeping a lazy line up my back. "Oh, yeah? Something distracting you?"

We haven't talked about this. Haven't spoken about public office displays of affection. Would Simone even condone fraternization in the workplace?

Turning to face him, I grip my desk's edge. "Incredibly," I breathe out, trying desperately not to surround it with a moan.

Axel stays put, but his eyes pan from my lips to my breasts and back to my face. "The fact we—haven't typed a word for the story?"

His expressions and actions tell me his mind is *not* on the story either, but this time, we're not alone in the office. The thought has my gaze cutting to Axel's desk, recalling how he'd sat on it with his legs wide open, beckoning me. I rub my nails down my throat until Axel clears his throat, snapping me back to reality.

"Yes, the story. Absolutely." I nod once and return to the monitor, pulling up a Word doc. "Which one of us should type?"

Axel steps away, and I suppress a whimper from the empty feeling behind me when he's no longer there. He turns seconds later, wheeling his desk chair to position beside mine. "I don't need proof to know you're the faster typist of the two of us. Do you mind?"

Grinning, I take a seat and crack my knuckles. "Not at all. But please tell me you're not one of those types that use only two fingers on the keyboard?" I lift both index fingers and mime typing in mid-air.

"Thankfully, no. It'd take me forever and a day to write a column if that were the case. But I might do it now and again if writing a byline or something. Why risk hand cramps, right?" Axel splays his fingers and wiggles them.

I smile at him, and we pause, taking a moment to drink each other in with longing gazes. "I say we jump right into the start of the hockey game ten years later. Show our heroine at the game and smack the readers with the back story once she recognizes her ex on the enemy team."

Axel sneaks a hand under the desk and, incognito, squeezes my thigh before retreating back to his lap. "Sounds good. Now, how close are her seats? You remember the first game we went to? That far back, even a little closer, would be hard to make out their faces."

"Hm." I rest my elbows on the desk and steeple my fingers, tapping them against my lips. "Even when we were super close at the Hawks game, the helmets, the visors over their eyes, and constant movement make it hard, too."

"The way I see it—" Axel leans his forearms on my desk. Heat radiates from his skin like a roaring fire, and I find myself edging my elbow closer to siphon some of its warmth. "—you can either have them sitting directly behind the enemy bench—"

Confused, I cut him off. "Why would anyone want to sit behind the *enemy* bench?"

"Mostly to heckle the team." Axel snickers. "They like to beat on the glass, yell insults, try to distract the players."

"Does that actually work?" I bump my foot against his beneath the guise of my desk.

He runs the tip of his boot up my calf, and my elbow rolls off the desk, making me yelp. Grinning at his victory, he moves his foot to a safe distance again. "Nah. You get immune to it after the first few games, and it becomes white noise. You also have so much adrenaline going, your singular focus zeroes in on the game itself."

"Interesting. I interrupted. Sorry. What was the other thing you were going to say?" Without thinking it through, I pat his bicep. It's so firm and bulky in my tiny, frail hand I have to physically push my chair away from him using my foot not to grope him further.

Axel's gaze darkens, and he stares at the spot I touched before raking a hand through his hair as if he too needed to force himself to concentrate. "You could always have him and some other dude get into a fight. They tear off their gloves, whip off their helmets, and throw punches. They always show it on the jumbotron."

My spine zips straight, and I bounce in my seat, already typing the opening paragraph. "He'd be unmistakable at that point. I love it. And a fistfight? That's hot."

Axel leans back in his chair, shaking his head. "Do women really find the idea of two guys beating the piss out of each other attractive?"

"Why not? It boils down to our ancestral roots and animalistic sides where the males fought each other to prove their worth for a mate." I hit the period button with an exaggerated hand snap. "Did you ever get into a hockey fistfight?"

"Tons. I was a defenseman. Came with the territory." He leans past me and points at the screen where I'd already written an entire first page. "Did you type all of that from our three-minute conversation?"

Tons? Axel Nord on skates, defending his team's goal by physically fighting an opposing player? There's no doubt in my mind Axel rarely lost, and the very idea of it has my knees pinching together.

"Hm? What? Yes. You're inspiring. What can I say?" I rest my cheek in my hand and smile at him while batting my eyelashes.

He bops my nose with one finger and juts his head at the screen. "Let's keep going then. We could have this whole thing done by end of business day."

We don't complete the entire piece but get it well past the halfway point with me typing up a fury and Axel lending to the story with his hockey knowledge and know-how. We also manage to include aspects from our interviewees and unabashedly squeeze in a scene or two from *our* blossoming story. Not to exclude an almost kiss amidst skating, only to be interrupted by the Zamboni.

"Whew. Okay, I've been holding it in for the past hour, but I *need* to use the little girl's room. It's an emergency at this point." I lock my computer and jolt from my chair.

Axel pokes my side as I pass, tickling me and grinning like a jackal. I yelp and bat his hands away, shrieking about peeing myself. I head to the restroom, go about my business, wash my hands, and when I head back to my desk, ready to wrap up the work for the day with Axel, he's nowhere to be seen.

A peculiar unease tightens my chest, and I take a step forward. Why am I suddenly so insecure? He could be getting a coffee, or going to the bathroom himself, or maybe he's realized how silly and awkward I am and hid under his desk.

Rolling my eyes at my truly scatteredbrained activity, I shuffle down the hall, but pause when I hear Axel's voice—from Simone's office. Now, I've never been one to eavesdrop, and I know from the countless stories I've written it's *never* a good idea. So I have no idea why I decide to do it anyway, against my better judgment.

I push a hand against the corner wall to steady myself and lean enough to hear them clearly without revealing myself.

"And you're sure you want to do it this way?" Simone asks.

"Absolutely. It'd be easier and more efficient if I do it alone."

"Have you talked to Romance about this?"

What? Talked to me about what? And what the hell does he mean by doing it alone?

"No. I don't think we should. No reason to risk creativity."

I pant like I'd run several miles, my hand becoming so clammy it slides down the wall.

"Alright then, Sports. Consider the article yours."

Oh my—*no*. Axel wouldn't do this. He wouldn't. Do. This. Would he? The kisses, the flirting, the understanding? Can it all be a ruse? A distraction?

I clamp my hands over my mouth to douse the sound of sobs slowly forcing its way out. It can't be happening again. But I'd heard it plain as day.

Axel convinced Simone to headline the story—*our* story. So *he* can be the sole author of it.

TWELVE

AXEL

THE EASE WITH which Theo writes scenes once the inspiration sparks is truly a sight to behold. And her typing speed? I swear the woman has Kryptonian Supergirl blood in her veins or something. She's been this fresh, brightened drop of morning dew kissed by the sunlight since I met her, peeking through the elevator doors. But when she's writing? Her brightness blossoms to full-blown bursts of radiance. As if I could be *any* more attracted to her. This is why, after spending only a minute mulling over my decision, I make a beeline for Simone's office once Theo is preoccupied in the restroom.

Simone's door is cracked open, and I knock. "Simone? Do you have a moment?"

Simone remains laser-focused on paperwork organized in several neat stacks on her desk before tearing her gaze away for the few seconds it takes to see who's at her doorway. "Oh, Sports. Come in. Have a seat."

Running my hands through my hair, I step in and close the door behind me but leave it open a crack. I squeeze into one of two chairs facing her desk, scooting it back to make room for my knees and interlacing my hands on my stomach. "I have a proposition for you."

Suddenly, I have Simone's attention, and one of her thin brows arches to the ceiling. Her eyes go hooded, and the air in the room becomes dank and strangling.

I fan my palms at her and cough into my fist. "Not *that* kind of proposition. Though you are a charming woman."

I've never been the type to fumble over words, but here we are. Theodora Hackett strikes again, utterly clueless to the power she wields.

Simone appears disappointed for a heartbeat before her gaze is back on her papers. "Out with it, Sports."

"While I applaud your efforts teaming me and Theo up for this holiday sports piece." I scoot to the edge of my chair and rest my forearms on her desk, garnering more of her attention. I continue when she looks first to my limbs and finally to my face. "But let's be honest. I have no place writing romance. I can't say I've *ever* read a romance book."

Simone lets out a deep "I don't have time for this nonsense sigh," and slaps her pen to the desk. "Get to your point, Sports."

"Theo is immensely talented, and I want to elect not to have my name on the byline." I lift a gracious finger to halt Simone when she goes to speak. "I'll still help with hockey references and quality check, but this should come from her. She's proud of it, and it should *all* be hers."

Simone leans on one armrest, her expression melting into one that, if I were in a fantasy movie, would have me running for the hills from fear of being incinerated. "Let me get this straight." She pushes her fingertips together. "We agreed to hire you early to work on this piece specifically, and now you're asking to bow out?"

I mentally wince at this.

"Not at all. Theo gets the romance piece with me as a ghost co-writer, and I'll give you a holiday hockey article that's all fact and no fiction. You'll get two pieces out of this instead of one." The confidence I feel is soaring because what editor in their right mind could refuse this? I lean back and retreat to my aloof posture.

Simone taps a fingernail on one stack of papers and clicks her tongue against the back of her teeth. "A romance story and sports article coinciding with it. Encouraging couples to read together and possibly even educating those interested to learn more about the sport."

"Exactly. We could also get some photos of the athletes and include them if you ever intended to publish it physically." I'm on top of the world now and recline in my chair a tad, utterly relaxed.

"A centerfold. I like it." Simone nods, her eyes brightening now. "And you're sure you want to do it this way?"

"Absolutely. It'd be easier and more efficient if I do it alone."

Simone shifts in her seat, folding her hands atop the desk. "Have you talked to Romance about this?"

Have I talked to her about it? There wasn't time to stew on it, let alone run it by her first. And this is nothing if entirely in favor of *her*.

"No. I don't think we should. No reason to risk creativity."

A feline grin pulls at Simone's lips before she extends her hand. "Alright then, Sports. Consider the article yours."

Inside, I'm jumping like I'm in the middle of a Metallica concert mosh pit.

"You won't regret this, Simone." After shaking her hand and thanking her more than necessary, I enter the hall.

Theo's shoving things into her bag at her desk like someone's pulled the fire alarm. I flick my wrist to check the time. It's only five before four.

With my hands in my pockets, I sidle beside her, raising a brow when she jumps at the sight of me and yelps. "Where are you going, Romance?"

"Home," she clips, attempting to shove four notebooks stacked at different angles into the bag, grunting as she does so.

I juggle a stray paperclip resting in my pocket with two fingers. "There's still an hour left in the work day. Figured we might do some overtime to get this thing hammered out. Call it done?"

Theo vigorously shakes her head, making fiery tresses fan over her eyes. "Nope. Can't. I uh—remembered I need to pick up my dry cleaning."

What in the flying hell is going on? Did something happen in the ten minutes she went to the restroom?

"And you can't pick it up on your way to work tomorrow instead? It *has* to be tonight?" I bend sideways, trying to catch her gaze, but she lets the hair remain over her face and makes all effort *not* to look at me.

"No. I cannot, Axel. Otherwise, I wouldn't have anything to wear tomorrow." With the notebooks victorious, refusing to go in her bag, she flops them to the desk.

I scratch my cheek. How did our dynamic change so lightning fast? Yesterday, we shared a moment under that office tree, admitting we're on the same level when it comes to Christmas. Not only did we feel comfortable enough to tell each other this sensitive piece of information, but we have the *same* opinion on it. And now, she's acting as if I'm Krampus here to punish her for misbehaving and avoiding me to prevent it.

"Okay, then. See you tomorrow?" My mind is the world's most chaotic vehicle roundabout—circling and circling with no exit in sight.

Theo fumbles with her gloves, not caring that two fingers go into the same hole. After pulling her blue knit hat so tight to her head it covers her eyebrows, she breezes past me with a blunt, "Yup," emphasizing the "p" sound.

I stare down the hall as she disappears from view, standing motionless and numb. My phone buzzes across my desk and Spencer's face lights the screen. I wouldn't bother to answer if it had been anyone else, but Spence? He's precisely who I need right now and I swipe the screen to answer.

"Hey. You busy?" I ask.

Spencer's silent for a beat before chuckling. "You had me thinking for a moment that you called *me* and not the other way around."

"Sorry." I trace a pattern on my desk where I'd sat last night with Theo between my legs. "Some things have recently happened, and I'm feeling a little *forvirret*."

"I have no idea what that word means, but do know when you start dropping Norwegian, your head is anywhere but here. Ironically, I was calling to ask if you wanted to come over to watch the Meteors game tonight."

The Meteors. Since living on the East Coast, Spencer's been loyal to that hockey team and refuses to switch to the Hawks.

"Sure. But don't expect me to root for them." Cradling the phone with my shoulder, I slip on my jacket.

"Aw, come on. They're not playing the Hawks."

Some random commercial about hemorrhoid cream plays faintly in the background from his television.

Smirking, because laughing feels about as suitable as a root canal, I wave at Simone through her office window before exiting the office. "I'll be there in twenty, Spence."

"Great. I'll have a cold one waiting for ya, Ax."

Spencer lives only one block past where I do, so I make it a point to walk. As much as icy cold temperatures are associated with sickness, cold also has healing properties if you let it. Albeit generally in the form of plunging into icy waters, the frigid air always seems to work for me, too. Inside, I feel numb, so making my face feel the same, balances me. Though, it does nothing for my mental state.

Had I said something, *done* something? And why wouldn't she *talk* to me about it?

Have Yourself a Merry Little Christmas plays from a nearby shop with its door cracked, children run circles on the sidewalk while a woman stares at her phone screen, and scents of cinnamon overlap with the burning rubber from traffic, making nausea bubble in my gut. When I walk these streets with Theo, all I can smell is the holidays. There could be a rotting rat carcass trailing us, and I'd still only get whiffs of cinnamon, baked cookies, and juniper.

When Spencer answers his apartment door, my hands are in my jacket pockets, my head held low, and my gaze burns a hole in the swirly red carpet.

"Jesus, Ax. You look like hell," Spence announces, clapping a shoulder on my back and yanking me into the apartment.

"I certainly feel like it," I mumble, not bothering to take my jacket off, but toe my boots off, out of respect for his immaculate white carpet.

Spencer is in the kitchen, walking back with a brown bottle, and handing it to me. "Here. Plenty more where that came from and harder stuff in the cabinet if you need it."

Condensation formed on the bottle collects on my skin as I

wrap my hand around it. "Thanks."

"Okay, Nord. Now I *know* there's something going on because you haven't made one crack against the caterpillar growing on my upper lip."

Finally lifting my gaze, I spy the thin peppering of dark hair forming on Spencer's lip and bite the inside of my cheek. "Freddie Mercury called—" I start, losing my train of thought, completely forgetting where I intended to go with that joke.

Spencer sighs and takes the bottle from me. "Take off your damn coat, and let's go sit down. Come on, Axel, one arm then the other."

I do as he instructs, take the bottle back, and we sit on Spencer's brown leather sofa at opposite sides. "I like her, Spence." The words are vague and random, and I don't care.

"No shit, Sherlock." Spencer smirks and curls two fingers around the bottle's neck, swigging some beer and halfway watching the game.

"How do you know who I'm talking about?" I guzzle half the bottle.

"Theo?"

My shoulders slump, and I groan. "That'd be the one."

"What happened?" Spencer scoops the remote in his hand, muting the TV.

Did he just—mute a Meteors game? *Faen.*

"Am I coming across so pathetic you're muting the game?" I toss the empty beer bottle between my hands.

Spencer hikes one knee on the couch, turning to face me. "Yes. You do. Now talk."

It's one thing I always liked about Spence. No sugarcoating, no analogies. Straight to the point to resolve the problem.

"Things have been going great. She does *not* hate me, after all. Yes. You were right before you hold that one over my head." I eye Spencer sidelong, and he's grinning. "I mean, hell, Spence. We almost screwed in the office last night."

Still holding the bottle, he points at me. "Is that what this is about? She rejected you?"

Somehow, her ignoring me is far worse than any form of rejection. At least with rejection, it's a defined answer. There are no hopes and dreams wrapped in a decline. As much as it might hurt, at least you *know*.

"No. And I don't think she would have. Everything was going great. We'd just walked along Lake Shore Drive and had this mind-blowing kiss." I let my head fall back to the couch cushions. "Decided to pull an all-nighter feeling inspired for the story. And it was epically perfect. The only lights on were the tree, not a soul in sight." My hand grips the empty bottle so tightly my skin squeaks against the glass.

Spencer appears beside me, gently but forcibly removing the bottle from my grasp. "Let me grab you something that'll put more hair on your chest, hm?"

As Spencer disappears to the kitchen, I sit forward with my arms on my thighs, face falling into my palms. "The damn janitor walked in on us, Spence."

"Oh, yikes. How far had you two gotten?" Spencer yells from the kitchen, the sounds of ice clanking into a glass following.

It could've been worse. So much worse.

"Thankfully, all of our clothes were still on, but hell, I pushed it with that stunt. Especially being the new guy. What if that would've been my boss?" Hearing Spencer's sock-clad feet brushing the carpet, I lift my head.

"You're detouring here." Spencer wiggles a tumbler glass in front of my face. "What's the real reason for the doom and gloom? Because you can easily start things up again in a more private setting if she was that ready for it in the first place."

Heat rushes to my face, and I rub the glass over my forehead, wincing. "We were on a roll today. Got nearly the entire column done. Then she goes to the damn bathroom and comes back a completely different person."

"Hm." Spencer glances at the television where the Meteors are losing zero to five and promptly turns it off. "Did someone say something to her? Did she get a phone call with some bad news?"

"I have no idea." I sip the drink—scotch it tastes like. "She wouldn't talk to me. Wouldn't even *look* at me."

Spencer's finger taps against the bottle, and he rests it on his knee. "Strange. And where were you while she was in the bathroom?"

With that, Spencer goes into lawyer mode.

"I went to talk to Simone." I take another sip, only this time it's a hard swallow—one that holds the alcohol in my throat long enough to create a dull burn before going down the rest of the way.

"Care to elaborate there, slick?"

Cough sputtering, I notice Spencer's mustache for the first time. "You look like that one villain from the Rocky and Bullwinkle show with that thing." I point at his mouth.

"We can discuss my poor mustache-growing genes later, Ax. What were you talking to Simone about?" Spencer snaps his fingers at me, forcing me to focus on him.

"I proposed a different plan for the article. To give Theo full creative control with me still handling the legitimacy of anything hockey-related, and take me off the byline." I shrug because this really doesn't seem like a big deal to me when, in retrospect, it's benefiting Theo most of all.

Spencer raises a finger. "Let me guess. You didn't run this by Theo first? Assumed she'd be delighted about it?"

My eyes form such fierce slits Spencer becomes a blur. "Why wouldn't she be?"

"Ah, my man. Not saying she wouldn't, but you two are supposed to be *partners*, and now you've gone behind her back even if it *were* for something positive." Spencer hisses at his phone displaying the game's final score: five to one. He reaches a hand over his shoulder and yanks the Meteors jersey off, throwing it in a slump in the space between us.

"Okay, let's say you're right. That doesn't explain why she'd already be pissed about it. She doesn't know I talked to her." The skin below one eye twitches. "You don't think she has telepathy, do you?"

Spencer chuckles and adjusts his wrinkled white undershirt now that the jersey is gone. "You are a stallion when casually dating women, but become a damn-right pony when you *like* one of them. Know that?"

Tilting my head back, I down the rest of my drink. "We were doing so well without analogies, Spence."

"I don't know, dude." Spencer ruffles his hair. "Maybe a co-worker overheard part of your conversation with Simone and spilled the beans to her before you got back to your desk."

Both Desiree and Rupert are loyal to a fault with Theo. It makes sense they would have her best interests at heart. But did my stance on it hold no value?

"Possibly," I whisper. There's no chance in hell of getting much sleep tonight.

"Tomorrow, come right out and ask her if that's the issue and set the record straight. Sounds simple enough to me."

"But what if that isn't the problem? Then I need to deal with what *is* the problem *and* a new one once she finds out I didn't consult with her first?" A dull ache forms between my eyes, and I rub my thumb there.

Spencer stands, holding out his hand for my empty glass. "You're making this more complicated than it has to be. Ninety percent of the world's problems are either miscommunication or lack thereof. I see it every time I walk into that courtroom, friend." He takes my tumbler to the kitchen, the ice jangling against the sink as he dumps it.

"Thanks for listening to me whining," I mumble, standing from the couch and stretching my arms skyward.

Spencer leans his hands on the couch's back. "I know whining, and that wasn't it. We all need help navigating life sometimes. And you'll be there for me when I need it. Otherwise, I'd have told your sorry ass to figure it out." Spencer smirks and punches my shoulder. "You wanna crash here tonight?"

Being somewhere else besides home may help keep my thoughts at a simmer versus a full boil. Either way, it's worth a shot.

"You mind? I'll dip out early to shower and change for work at home."

Spencer pats the couch. "Don't mind at all. Let me grab you a pillow.

I take my jacket resting on the armrest and fold it over a chair, letting an exhale push from my nose.

"Here you go." Spencer tosses the pillow to the couch after fluffing it. "You can use this blanket on the back here if your Norse ass gets cold."

"Thanks, Spence. And I mean that." I use my knuckles to knead my opposite palm. Being vulnerable like this in front of your best friend isn't always the most comfortable.

"Don't mention it. Hope you can manage at least two winks of shuteye with all that going on in your head." Spencer smirks, shaking his head, and turns to walk away.

"Don't think we're done talking about that furry comb you have on your upper lip," I say to his back.

Spencer glares at me over his shoulder. "Sticks and stones. I hope you like wearing bright red on your head."

I manage a laugh—a short burst followed immediately by a frown. Once Spencer's bedroom door shuts, I move to the floor lamp and turn off the light, spilling darkness over the room. After sitting on the couch and staring at fuzzy shadowed outlines of Spencer's belongings, I lift my feet and lay back. I try to calm my mind, count my breaths, and focus on each bone, starting at my toes, but nothing keeps the thoughts from consuming me.

Have I somehow lost Theo before ever gaining a chance to *have* her?

THIRTEEN

THEODORA

NO SOONER DO I overhear their conversation, I grab my jacket and head straight home. Did I lock my computer? Ugh. Hopefully, Desiree covers for me if I didn't, but I can't stay here. I can't risk co-workers seeing me cry, or Simone, or worse—Axel. My ex royally screwing me over in far more ways than I care to remember hasn't been a thought in over a year. Lucky me that such a trivial thing as a three-sentence conversation can catapult me straight over the proverbial cliff.

I'm up the following day after what I calculated was approximately one hour of sleep through the night's tossing and turning, flopping to my back to stare at the ceiling and contemplate my life's choices, or the infamous brain that never shuts up. I manage to shower myself without issue, so we're winning in that regard, but as soon as I enter the office, it becomes a game of cat and mouse that is *not* of the endearing slow-burn variety. Axel tries to find me, and I avoid him at every possible turn. If Simone hadn't outlawed hoodies in the office space, I'd have worn one. *That* is the level we're at, folks.

How does one deal with this and still go about their work day? The last time, I quit my job and sought greener pastures. But also last time, he'd been my boyfriend of two years and not only weaseled his way into my story but managed to throw it in my face. Axel has been fairly mum about it thus far, so at least I know he's got an ounce of respect.

I'm going to the mailroom to make copies of whatever I managed to grab off my desk before scurrying away when Axel's head appears over the horizon of desks and cubicles. Gasping, I duck into the first available area—the break room.

Ah, yes. Coffee is perfect. This oasis will do nicely.

Grabbing my same beloved Darth Vader holiday mug, I pour caffeinated elixir into it while watching Axel through a crack in the blinds. He's sighing, rubbing his temples, and seemingly cursing to himself before whipping around to face his desk.

Hopefully, he's finally giving up on finding me because I'll crawl through the fire escape even if we *are* several floors up, *and* I'm terrified of heights. Some may think I'm being pathetic or taking things out of proportion, but it's a matter of self-preservation and protecting my heart.

I doctor up my coffee with creamer and start on the sugar packets, staring at Axel and all his smugness, glancing around him as if worried anyone else has caught on to his bull crap. My fixation warps into an expression that I'm certain resembles an agitated gremlin, and Desiree proves this theory when she walks past me, halts, and moonwalks back to the doorway.

She's in the room and now leaning into my face. "Theo? What's wrong with you?"

"Nothing." I rip open another packet, unblinking and unfaltering in my Axel stare down. "Why?"

Desiree blocks my Viking view and points down. "For starters, honey, you've got a dozen empty sugar packets lying on the table and are adding your thirteenth."

"Crap," I blurt, dropping the current sugar packet like a firecracker.

"What's going on with you, friend?" Des discreetly slides the coffee mug away from me and swooshes the empty packets into the garbage.

Shooting from the hip, I point at Axel through the window, my eyes squinting, widening, and back to squinting again. "He. And then she. And they. But *he*—"

I'm not making any sense, even to myself. And sound like someone who has lost all parts of speech save for pronouns and conjunctions.

Desiree's hand lightly rests on mine, and she lowers it. "You'll come with me to my next food critique site. I'll tell Simone I need your romantic perspective regarding the setting. Alright?"

I shake my head, stubbornly refusing to let Axel make me feel uncomfortable in my workplace, around coworkers and friends I considered family. But then, he's already done a bang-up job with that, hasn't he?

"Theo—" Des's hand grips under my chin, and she turns my face to hers. "It's at Scarpacci's."

A spark of hope rumbles in my stomach. There is no shortage of places to find deep-dish pizza in Chicago, but Scarpacci's has some of the best. Perfectly melted cheese. Adequate sauce amount and taste. And the best part? They don't put crumbles of meat on it. They cover the entire thing with one slab, ensuring every bite is bursting with flavor. This woman knows the way straight to my heart through my stomach.

"Fine. I suppose I can suffer through a free lunch with my bestie at the expense of wallowing in self-pity at work and playing Dodge the Viking." I twirl my wrist and flick something from my nail.

"That's the spirit. And you'll tell me what happened with you and Axel so that you can stop looking like an agent on a stakeout who never intends on pursuing their mark. Okay?" She ushers me toward the door, massaging my shoulders.

Moments later, we're sitting at a corner table in Scarpacci's, the lighting moody and dim, with most of the illumination from the artificial fire table sconces. I trail my fingers over the red and white checkered tablecloth, dryness coating my throat, knowing what comes next.

Desiree orders us each a personal-sized deep-dish pizza, and I'm thankful to have lunch for the next two days. Despite its labeling as "personal-sized," they are still big enough and loaded with so many ingredients that most end up eating only one portion of it and carting the rest home in a doggy bag.

"With how long Scarpacci's has been in business, I'm surprised the magazine has you covering here," I say with genuine curiosity and only marginally as a deterrent.

"They're under new management. Now—" Desiree states this with such flippancy that I want to slap my palms on the table but decide on decorum instead.

"Wait. New management? That means the recipe could've changed." I grip the table's sides. "It could taste entirely different. I'm unsure if I'm ready for this type of world-rocking right now, Des. I—"

Her foot kicks my calf underneath the table, not with the brute force of an MMA fighter, but enough to make me gape at her. "Focus, Hackett. Tell me what's going on."

This is a can of worms I'd hoped to leave buried in the ground, rotting until each worm became a shriveled, dried-up, non-existent speck in the universe.

"I never told you about the last guy I dated. I mean, dated seriously." Yanking the paper ring from the napkin in front of me, I begin tearing it into microscopic pieces. "We'd been dating for a couple of years. He was a fellow writer at my local newspaper before Celestial. He covered most of the artsy fartsy happenings in the area."

Desiree lets out a breath like a deflating puffer fish and leans back. "Oh, man. I can already guess where this is going." A frown pulls at her lips, and I can appreciate this expression because she's constantly reminded me how such mouth movements can cause wrinkles.

"Our editor asked me to go to this Shakespeare event they were having and write not only about the event but the romance vibes in the air." A snow pile of white paper rests on the table now and I swirl my finger in it. "He thought me better suited for the task given my aptitude for flowery prose." I smirk, remembering this and how absurd it sounded at the time, but now would take the compliment and frame it in hindsight.

Desiree remains silent, even when the waiter brings glasses of red wine. She picks one up and swirls its contents. Taking a tiny bit in her mouth, she tastes it and nods to herself as if making a mental note instead of physically jotting it down straight away.

"So, I worked the piece, took photos, did interviews, and wrote one of the better straight-laced articles of my career." My sinuses sting, but never being a fan of crying in public, I gulp the threatening tears away.

"Did that asshole seriously steal it somehow?" Desiree's frown deepens, a crinkle forming in her brow.

A laugh pushes from my throat—but not out of amusement or the kind you do when you're so in pain and don't know what else to do—no, this one is a laugh at the absurdity of it all. "Yes. Yes, he did. I'm still unsure how he convinced our editor that we'd partnered on it. He straight lied that he had enough input to call it his article. And it's all because I asked him *one* question." I make a fist and smoosh the paper pile until every piece is flattened. "But it was enough ammunition, he knew that I couldn't argue and say I didn't."

"Wow." Desiree taps her fingernails on the table in a jittery staccato. "I don't know this jerk, and I want to knee him in the balls."

"I'd have broken up with him over it and stayed at the paper because I loved the people I worked with, but when he stood in front of them all and blatantly took full credit for the piece—" Sighing, I focus my gaze on the green branches interwoven with holly and off-white lights bordering the rafters above us. "—I knew I couldn't make it work and put in my two weeks the next day."

"I'll say this much." Desiree reaches across the table and pats my hand. "I'm only glad because I met my best friend at Celestial Magazine when she came puttering in, all bright-eyed and disheartened. Now I know what was up with the latter."

Sniffling, I bite my lip and rest my other hand atop hers. "Always a silver lining, right?" Our pizzas arrive, and the tangy smell of tomato mingling with cheese, sausage, and crust has the corners of my mouth watering.

Desiree rests a notepad beside her plate, quickly scribbling something onto it. She takes a photo of the spread with her phone, picks up her fork, and raises it to me for us to clink together like toasting with glasses.

"I'll let you savor a bite of that before your mouth starts moving to explain why you were stammering like a broken record while simultaneously trying to overdose on sugar in the office." Desiree points at me with her fork before we both shovel heaping bites.

We are a mix of groans, moans, and all other noises far less suitable for a public restaurant. But with flavor like this, it's impossible not to vocalize your appreciation. Thankfully, the recipe hasn't changed a bit. I take far more chews than necessary, delaying the inevitable, and once I make an exaggerated gulp, Desiree's hand is on my plate, sliding it away from me.

I hold the fork poised for stabbing and stare at her hand. "Des?"

"Calm down, Aquaman. I'll let you have a bite for every piece of information you divulge. Deal?" Des licks her lips and writes something on her notepad.

"Your evil bargaining prowess with pizza is unmatched."

The crooning, melancholy tones of *Please Come Home for Christmas* by Eagles play over the loudspeakers. Ironic. The volume makes it just faint enough to cause an irritated pang in the back of my skull.

"Axel and I have grown—closer," I start, mentally patting myself on the back for saying *something*, anything, despite being lured with delicious meat pie.

Desiree pulls a bite from her pizza, purposefully making the cheese go stringy as she lifts it above her head. "Nuh-uh. You don't get a bite for that. We *all* knew that."

Snarling, I cross my ankles and slide them beneath my seat. "We've kissed. More than once. With tongue."

Desiree chokes on pizza and reaches for her wine, coaxing it down the right pipe. "When the hell did this happen?"

"The practice day before the actual hockey game? He was there ice skating and—" Desiree shoves the plate to me, and I stab my fork into it like a starving chimpanzee, scooping it into my mouth before she can take it away.

"He skates?" Desiree's brow bobs with intrigue.

Nodding and shoving the food to one side of my mouth for safekeeping, I drape a hand over my lips and mumble, "Mmhm. He used to play hockey."

Desiree taps the crust on her pizza. "Well, he certainly keeps getting more appealing, doesn't he?"

I cease chewing and throw her an exasperated glare.

"Sorry. Please continue."

The sauce has collected at the corner of my mouth, and I dab it away with a napkin. "We almost kissed there, *did* kiss when they put us on the Kiss Cam the next day, and—"

"Confession?" Desiree quickly and repeatedly clicks and unclicks her pen. "My acting completely surprised about several kisses was well—untrue. Rupert told me about the Kiss Cam." She flinches like I'm preparing to throw gooey cheese and sauce in her direction.

Though it's tempting, this pizza is far too tasty for such frivolous acts.

"Of course, he did. He can be a real cackling hen, that one." I twirl my fork into a stray piece of cheese and eat only it as my next bite.

"Aw, don't be mad at him. He was bursting with excitement. He had to tell someone and swore me to secrecy." A wicked glint to put the Evil Queen to shame flashes in her gaze. "He said it looked pretty steamy before the camera cut away."

A shuddering breath leaves my lungs, and I fork more pizza into my mouth to mask the way my traitorous hormones have not forgotten, nor care about, Axel's conniving ways. "It did," I ramble around my cheesy bite of pizza.

"I guess I'm confused. It sounds like you two are hitting it off. This is amazing for you. And—" Desiree cups her wine glass, lifting it to me before sipping. "—he works with you, so you don't have the career bit as an excuse."

And now I'm reminded of how lovely everything is until this wrench in the holiday pie.

"We had a breathtaking kiss near the lake. It was even snowing. Pulled a late night in the office to write and ended up just— talking, but then—"

The words rumble through my brain: "It'd be more efficient if I do it alone." "No. I don't think we should." "Consider the article yours."

"Theo?" Desiree's voice is wistful and laced with concern.

"It's happening again, Des. Axel is trying to take credit for the story. *Just* like my ex." When I lift my gaze to hers, I expect to find a BFF fuming, ready to raise torches and pitchforks and storm Axel's apartment. But what do I see? She stares at me in disbelief, shaking her head. "What? Why are you looking at me like that?"

"Because something's not right here. How do you know, or what happened to make you think this is the case?" Desiree rests her fork on her plate, finished.

For whatever reason, I go on the defense. I heard what I heard.

"Des, I *heard* him talking to Simone in her office." I point downward and poke my finger against the table.

Desiree searches my face as if looking for the one clue to unravel this all. "Did you hear the entire conversation?"

Why do friends always ask the right questions that make your head spin?

"I don't know. How could I know?" Brushing crumbs from the table, I flop back to my chair.

"So, you're making the lavish accusation that Axel is trying to steal the story for himself out of what *could* have been a partial conversation?" Desiree writes on her notepad, and if it isn't about deep-dish pizza, I'll throw it straight into the Chicago River.

"He said it'd be more efficient to go about it *alone*. And in the end, Simone said that article was *his*." I find myself sitting straighter now, making some politician-like hand gesture to emphasize my point further.

Desiree quiets and chews her thumbnail. If she were standing, I imagine she'd be pacing the length of the room like a homicide detective attempting to piece it all together at a crime scene. "That does sound suspect, but I think something is missing. You know more about Axel than I do. Does he seem like the type to betray that quickly? That easily? He *just* started at the magazine."

The short time I've known Axel already feels more like years. And this realization could be the part that scares me the most.

"You have a point, though. Simone hates signs of weakness. And someone coming to her ready to oust another employee in his first week?" I rest my chin on my hand and whine. "Why does this have to be so hard?"

"What does? Life?" Desiree cackles and slaps the table. "Look, girly. You need to pull your big girl pants on and have an adult conversation with him. Talk. To. Him."

It's true. I feel juvenile and childish about this entire thing.

"But what if I'm right?"

Desiree shrugs one shoulder. "Then you'll know, and you can go to Simone to get his ass canned."

"That's a little harsh, don't you think?"

"Why?" Desiree flags a waiter. "If he *is* the type to go behind someone's back, are you telling me you'd want to work with him again, let alone continue to fool around with him?"

I bunch my shirt in my hand, hating the idea of never kissing Axel again. Not feeling his fingertips against my skin. Not ever experiencing what it'd be like to experience *all* of him. "And if I'm wrong?" My gaze bounces to Des's, desperation and exhaustion obvious, and I didn't try to hide it.

"Then he'll either not be able to get past it, or he will, and you two will have a big ol' laugh over it and jump in the sack." Desiree offers a sympathetic smile that makes me shrink to the size of a field mouse.

"Yeah," I whisper, grabbing the Styrofoam to-go box the waiter rests by my pizza and boxing it up.

"Be right back. Going to thank the new manager, and we'll walk home, kay?" Desiree stands, still smiling, and whisks away.

I stare so long at the table the checkered pattern begins to animate. The lines move left to right, boxes overlapping. It's enough to have me closing my eyes, dizziness making me topple in my chair. A hand rests on my shoulder, and I jump, kicking my chair back.

Desiree fans her palm at me. "You're incredibly jumpy."

"Sorry. I think I got a grand total of sixty minutes of sleep last night." I fumble putting on my jacket.

"I can imagine. Let's get you home. Hopefully, our conversation will let you rest better, hm?" Des rubs between my shoulder blades.

"You better be leaving a good review for this place. Don't need the advertisement of a new owner to steer people away."

We move to the icy winds outside, and shove our hands in our jacket pockets.

"It's mostly good. I had to be honest and say they burnt the crust on one side." Desiree winces with one eye.

"What? But people hardly ever eat that part of the crust," I shout.

Desiree laughs, causing bursts of warm air mixed with the

cold swirling between us. "Calm down. I told the owner it was probably a matter of installing new heating coils in one of the ovens because *your* pizza was fine. And I told him if he did that and invites me back once he does, I'll wait on publishing to give him a fair chance."

Beaming over flipping deep-dish pizza that, apparently, I'll stand on a soap box for like a darn preacher, I curl to Desiree's side and hug her. "Thank you."

We part ways at the one street that separates our apartment buildings, and I'm halfway through my door when my phone buzzes with an incoming text. My heart throttles against my chest, hoping somehow it's Axel. This tells me a lot more than I'm willing to admit. But turning on my screen reveals not a text from Axel but a group text from Mary:

Mary: Hello, co-workers! Don't forget that tomorrow is the annual office Christmas party! You don't have to wear an ugly sweater, but please do wear something festive in green and red so we really bring out the cheer. Have a great day!

The party. I can easily pretend I'm sick and avoid both it and Axel and the whole freaking thing, but—no. I enjoy these parties and won't let someone take that from me, even if they wind up being a manipulative *cotton-headed ninny muggins.*

FOURTEEN

AXEL

TO SAY I tried to follow Spencer's advice would be a gross understatement. I made every attempt possible to talk things out with Theo, but she clearly had it in her mind that she, too, would try anything imaginable to *stay* away from me. I wish I was kidding. As soon as she'd waltzed into the office, with her hair hanging over her face like I wouldn't recognize those fiery tresses, she zoomed past her desk and busied herself elsewhere. For an hour, she didn't even bother to take off her jacket.

For a brief moment, it became amusing, watching her duck in and out of places like a prairie dog checking if the coast was clear. Had she really thought I didn't see her? Well, I *had* and fought every compulsion not to lock gazes with her and give away my apparent upper hand. I could've been more brash with my desire to speak with her, but if she was that adamant? I also didn't want to make her uncomfortable. Especially when every time I did seem to draw nearer to her, she skittered away like a startled wild mare.

And all hope flew straight out the window when she and Desiree left the office and never came back. The final click on the hanging wall clock as the big hand reached twelve and the little one moved to five sounded louder than usual that day alone.

But today is another day. Because today is the office holiday party and as good of an opportunity as any to finally get her to talk to me. To tell me what I did or what I said to make her suddenly act so aloof toward me. The level at which it's been driving me insane is all too telling. I've felt it before, but never to this magnitude and never so—*quickly*. I'm falling for her. Pure and simple. I'm falling for her something fierce.

I own nothing in either red or green in my wardrobe and stopped in my favorite men's clothing store while running errands earlier today. Never being a huge fan of the color red, aside from the Hawks, of course, I opted for what the clerk called a Henley shirt in "hunter green." I can't say I've ever bothered to learn what shades of green were meant to be called. As far as I'm concerned, there's light, dark, and neon green.

I stand in front of the mirror, slicking back my hair, tidying up my beard, and pushing the long sleeves up to my elbows. A glance at my watch reveals I better get my ass moving if I'm going to walk and get to the office in time. Something tells me Mary becomes a different person at these events. She's poured so much time and effort into it, and to have things go awry—example—

people showing up late, could make this other side of her come out. It's a hunch, but one I'd rather not test.

I grab my jacket, and my phone vibrates in my back jeans pocket. After slipping my arms into the coat sleeves, I look at the screen on my way out the door. Spencer. Of course.

Spencer: You talk to her yet?

Me: Nope. But not from a lack of trying.

Spencer: What's that supposed to mean?

I'm on the sidewalk now, passing traffic lights and tourists, simultaneously texting Spencer. It's a feat to multitask while avoiding bumping into droves of tourists flooding the streets.

Me: She's avoiding me. And succeeding.

Spencer: She's committed. I'll give her that.

Me: It's fine. The office holiday party starts in a few minutes.

Spencer: Ah ha. Perfect opportunity for that Nord charm, eh?

I smirk at this. Charming isn't a word I'd have ever thought to describe myself.

Me: Something like that. And I'm about to the building, so I'm going radio silent.

Spencer: Fill me in. Go get her, Grizzly.

I pause in front of the office building doors, arching a brow at my phone screen.

Me: Isn't it supposed to be "tiger."

Spencer: Sure, but you're more of a bear.

Shaking my head and not answering him, I mute my phone and shove it in my back pocket.

Mary has gone the extra mile setting up the office for this party. The typical decorations hang from desks and light fixtures, but she's added a ton more. It looks like a dozen garage's worth of storage contained decorations has exploded but organized to perfection. Even the plastic cups surrounding the ice sculpture punch bowl each have a different colored bow stuck to them.

My mind fixates on the overstimulation of my senses from so many color varieties, sparkling objects, and varying patterns, but my mind pushes past it all, determined to find one person in particular. My gaze pushes through the fog of glitter and holiday cheer, searching for the sole reason I decided to attend the party in the first place. But I come up empty. She's nowhere to be found, and my heart melts to my feet.

Mary clears her throat and stands in front of the crowd as if getting ready to make some formal announcement. She's wearing a red and green Christmas sweater with a t-rex on the front in a matching sweater, but the sleeves don't fit its short arms. She raises her hands, asking for the murmuring conversations to cease.

"Everyone, thank you so much for coming and taking the time to dress to the theme. You all look amazing. Especially you, Rob." Mary points at a man with spiky brown hair wearing a black sweater with alternating trees and goalie masks. A moose-shaped mug is in the center with a station wagon, mobile home, and the words *Fun, Old Fashioned Family Xmas. Christmas Vacation* is one of my absolute favorite holiday movies."

I roll my eyes and make for the punch bowl, inwardly hoping it's spiked.

"It's a pretty open forum tonight, folks. No crazy antics like Pin the Tail on the Reindeer or holiday-themed Twister or anything." Mary pauses for laughter that I know isn't as roaring as she planned for. "All I ask is to have fun, eat, drink, be merry. And please, *please* make use of the dancefloor. Enjoy, everyone!"

I nab a cup with a metallic blue bow attached and ladle some punch into it. After sipping, I breathe out a sigh. If there's alcohol in this, it's so little I could chug the entire bowl and not feel a buzz.

Rob, Mary's favorite sweater man, sidles beside me and pulls a flask from inside his jacket. "Won't tattle on me, will you?"

My gaze stays forward to keep watch, and I hold my cup behind my back. "Not if you give me a little snort of that."

"You bet," Rob says, laughing. "Mary's intentions are always so sound at these things but almost *too* pure for my tastes. She's a good kid, though."

"Yeah. And uh, thanks." I can't think of anything else to say because, to be frank, I don't give a rat's ass about Rob. Nor do I feel like making small talk with him. After lifting the cup to him in a gesture of gratitude, I shove one hand in my pocket and blend with the outskirts of the crowd.

Rockin' Around the Christmas Tree blasts from the DJ booth, and I try not to groan. Instead, I shove my nose in my cup and sip the alcoholic punch, thanks to Sweater Rob. Familiar scents have the hairs on my arm standing on end—cinnamon, vanilla, and pine. I immediately swivel, searching, hoping the source is her. It *has* to be her.

The fluorescent office lights turn off, rotating in red, green, and white lights replacing them, spinning, flashing, and strobing throughout the space. I see flowing red hair through the seas of bobbing bodies haphazardly dancing to the music, but when I reach that same spot, there's nothing.

I'm on full alert now, following the scent like a hound dog, flashes of auburn hair becoming mirages through the bouncing lights to the point I want to stop and roar her name. But I don't have to because the next turn I take collides us straight into each other.

Theo gasps and slaps a hand over her cup, keeping its contents from spilling. "Can you please watch where you're—" Her gaze lands on my chest, laughing at first, but her expression melts into shock as she realizes my eyes are much further up and who it is she bumped into. Desiree is at her side and she bears a similar expression.

"Can we talk?" My jaw tightens, and I direct the words straight at Theo.

Theo lifts her chin and taps her finger against her cup. "Des and I were in the middle of a crucial conversation."

"Nope. We're done. She's all yours." Desiree nudges Theo in my direction, giving her wide eyes.

Theo mouths something to her, but once Desiree is out of sight, she relents and turns back to me. "Axel, what are you doing here?"

She looks beautiful and adorable in her dark green dress, skirt billowing and falling to mid-thigh. The top hugs her curves and compliments her boobs, sleeves long but stopping right below her elbow.

"I do believe I work here, Theo. Or have you forgotten that, since you've been avoiding me the past thirty-six hours?" Taking a risk, I move my gaze away from her, pretending to glance around the room, and casually sip my drink as if her ignoring me hasn't bothered me.

She guffaws and drapes one arm across her stomach, sipping from the cup with her other hand, a light blue bow stuck to hers. "It's for good reason, and you *know* it."

Alright. It *is* something I did, but I have no clue as to what. It's a start?

"Honestly? I have no idea what you're talking about." I snap my gaze back to hers, scraping the callus on my right forefinger against my cup, waiting for her to elaborate.

She rolls her eyes so profusely that her neck follows. "Hey, look, Naomi's been eyeballing your backside for the past several minutes. Maybe you should talk to her. I'm sure she'd gladly go home with you tonight, Norseman."

My mouth begins to form the word "what," and the second I glance over my shoulder, Naomi has her groping hand on it, and Theo has disappeared. "Theo," I yell into the crowd, not caring if it's too loud or not.

"I'm over here coming onto you and you yell out someone else's name?" Naomi snickers, and pokes a bright red fingernail to my nose. "You *do* like playing hard to get."

Gently but with enough firmness to tell her I mean business, I take hold of Naomi's wrists. "Naomi, I'll tell you for the last time that I'm not interested. And just because this is a holiday party, not during work hours, doesn't mean that'll change a damn thing. Are we *clear*?"

Naomi blinks in disbelief, her petite arms twisting within my touch, and I let go, holding my palms up. "Jesus. Fine. Have it your way." She turns, making sure to slap me in the face with her hair as a final declaration of what she thinks of me.

Finally. How kind of her.

I'm pushing through co-workers, ignoring their grunts and yelps of protest. I spot Theo leaning against a wall away from everyone and chatting with Desiree. When Theo's gaze lands on me, I swear she looks elated that I'm sans Naomi and came looking for *her*. Or it could be my imagination running away with itself.

Desiree smiles at me and waves before nudging Theo's arm, urging her toward me.

Note to self: You owe Desiree a grand *Jul* gift.

Theo folds her arms in a huff when she lands in front of me, leaving two feet of space between us. She forces her gaze away and toward the tree—her lifeline, her calm.

"Theo, you'll have to level with me here." My cup is now empty, and I rest it on the nearest desk before throwing my arms out at my sides. "Lay it on me."

I expect her face to soften, for her to sigh and let it all out, but she does none of it. Instead, her jaw clenches, and her brow furrows to the point they nearly touch one another.

"Why do *I* have to be the one to tell *you* what you've done, Axel? I want to hear you *say* it." Theo rises to the balls of her silver high heels, points at me, and flops back down.

Frustration burrows in me like a frantic mole escaping a predator.

Last Christmas by Wham echoes in the space, and I don't hesitate to hold my hand out to her. "Dance with me, Theo."

Her arms are still crossed and pressed firmly to her chest, but her foot bounces, and she glances from my hand to my face and back again. "No."

"Please don't be stubborn. Not now. I *promise* there's an

explanation for whatever is going on. But I need you to enlighten me just a tad more." I re-emphasize my hand and wiggle my fingers like enticing worms luring a prized bass.

She sighs a harsh breath through her nostrils and takes my hand. "Fine. But we're keeping this middle school rated. Got it?"

I arch a brow, remembering middle school quite clearly. My first dance I'd made it to second base with a girl. She circles a space between us with her arms when I stay silent.

"Ah. Gotch ya. So, no dry humping then?" I half grin, wishing nothing more than to make her smile again, to make her face brighten with laughter.

"Axel," she warns, trying to turn away from me.

I hold her hand tighter, not letting her go for anything now that she's cracked, and I lead her to the floor. Ten others surround us, but she's the only one who exists. I take her hands and place them on my shoulders before resting mine on her hips. It feels silly and really like I *am* back in middle school, but ironically, it's so us I can't help but cherish it.

Theo's fingers pluck at each other behind my head. "I'm going to ask you something, and I need you to be honest with me because I'll know you're lying. Understand?"

"*Forstått*. Hit me with it."

She bites her lip when I speak Norsk but closes her eyes to refocus. "Are you trying to take the story, our holiday hockey story, for yourself?"

A boulder lands in my gut.

"What?" I breathe out, risking a step closer, but she stiff-arms me into staying at a distance. "I would never do that, Theo. *Why* would I do that?"

Theo snarls and lightly swats my shoulder before dropping her arms to her sides. "Axel, I told you *not* to lie to me."

"I'm not," I say a tad more haughtily than intended but blame it on my entire being going on the defense. "Where is this coming from, Romance? Hm?"

Mary clears her throat beside us, and I have half a mind to wonder if she's rented a teleporting machine because she popped in out of nowhere. "Hey, you two. Theo, I noticed you don't happen to be wearing any red?"

Theo glares at me and makes no motion to look at Mary. "My hair. That's red. Happy?" She sweeps some in my direction, but we're too far apart, and it misses me. Ha.

Mary forces a smile and turns her attention to me. "And Axel?"

Not caring Theo wants distance, I slide forward and lower my face to hers. "My. *Boxers*."

"Oh. Oh, uh, my," Mary says through a shaky voice.

Theo is still staring daggers into my inner soul, but there's no hiding the glance she makes below my navel, no doubt wondering if this, too, I was lying about.

"Okay. I fear my sweater catching on fire from the flaming tension between you two, and it is mostly made of polyester, so—" Mary snaps her fingers. "I'm going to let you two be."

"Is this your red flag, Axel?" Theo doesn't try to step away, allowing me to get so close we share the same breath. "Lying?"

"About—" I start, snaking my hand around her waist, ready to snap it away if she gives one hint she doesn't want it there, but she doesn't budge. "—what?" It comes out like a subdued growl from my very marrow. Slowly pulling her closer, my insides melt when her hands rest on my arms. I sway us again, bringing this dance to a high school level, the song flipping to *Baby, It's Cold Outside*.

She licks her lips, a desperate want for my truth playing in her gaze. "So, you're *not* trying to steal the story from me?"

"No, Theo. I would never do that." Without thinking and without my body giving me any sense of warning, I press a kiss to her forehead and rest my chin atop her head. "You're so passionate about your writing and this story in particular you've run away with, so why would I take that from you?"

Her hands grip my shirt, light sniffle sounds muffling against my chest. "But I—"

"Hey." I peel back and cup her chin. "Tell me, Romance."

Her eyes search mine, glistening with pending tears I hope won't escape and streak her cheeks. "I overheard you talking to Simone." Shame turns her cheeks rosy, and she looks away, but I coax her back.

"What exactly did you hear?"

She takes a long, deep breath through her nose, fighting back those same tears, and wraps her arms around my neck, still swaying with me. "That it would be more efficient if you did it alone, and Simone said the article was *yours*."

I couldn't have hoped for a better answer. Spencer was right. Again. This was all a misunderstanding.

A laugh pours from my stomach, puffing into her hair, and I hug her. "Oh, Theo."

"Why are you *laughing*?" Theo pushes against my chest, and I let her, but I'm still chuckling. "Seriously, Ax. This isn't funny."

"It kind of is." I shrug and take one of her hands in mine, keeping the other arm snaked around her. "Because you only heard the tail end of the conversation."

Her eyes widen as large as tree ball ornaments. "Why did she say the article was yours then? I don't understand."

"Let me clarify for you then." I move us around the dancefloor in the only two-person dance I know how to do—a waltz. She allows me to take the lead, and we sashay in a square together, pretending as if we were alone in the office after hours again.

"Please do," she whispers, that brightness I love about her slowly returning, starting at her eyes.

"I proposed to Simone that you get sole credit for the holiday romance. You on the byline and only you." I dip her.

Theo's head shoots up. "But we're supposed to be working *together*, and why didn't you tell me about this first?"

Point two for Spencer. Damn him.

"A piss poor move on my part, and I'm sorry. Truly. I thought it'd be a nice surprise when the story was published. I—" We're side-stepping back and forth for an eternity, and her palm presses to my cheek. "—I didn't want anything to ruin your mojo."

"I appreciate the thought, Ax, but what makes you think I yearn to see only my name on that byline?" She smiles so brightly I want to capture it in a mason jar like a firefly.

"I mean—why wouldn't you? That story is all you. I'm just the grunt who's giving you hockey advice." Chuckling, I hug her again, making silly, exaggerated turns and arm gestures now.

"You've given me so many ideas. I'm going to ask her to keep your name on it. Okay? Please?" Tears return to her eyes, but something tells me these are for an entirely different reason.

I press my forehead to hers, dying to kiss her, but I know it's not the time or place. "If you insist."

"But why did she say the article's yours?"

Kneading her palm between two of my fingers, I brush the hair from her face. "I offered to write a partner piece centered factually around hockey and family during the holidays using our interviews."

"I've—never been a part of a duo piece like that before." Theo's large green eyes blink up at me, fingers plucking together behind my neck. "Thanks for suggesting it to her."

"Theo, sweetheart," I whisper huskily. Pressing my lips to her ear, I say in only a decibel she can hear, "Spend the first night of *Jul* with me."

"When is it?" She leans back to look me in the eye.

"Tonight."

Theo's lips part as it slowly dawns on her what I'm asking—the implications of it. Yes, I want nothing more than to kiss, hug, screw her until the sunrise but I also truly crave to share traditions with someone again.

"I did promise you that I'd show you more traditions." I bump her cheek with a knuckle, grinning.

Theo's pupils dilate as if she's imagining what tonight may be like, and her finger traces her lip, followed by her teeth biting that same nail. "And where do you propose we spend this night?"

"Well, I have a fireplace and an incredible view of the skyline facing due *east*."

"East?" She cocks her head to one side. "Why does direction matter?"

"Because the entire point of the first night is to stay awake long enough to greet the sun." I squeeze her hands with mine, and instead of hesitation, Theo's grin widens.

"Alright. You leave first. I'll follow in a minute so it doesn't look *blatantly* obvious." Theo grips my shoulders, leaning in to kiss my cheek, but freezes. "Right. Go, go." She rushes me toward the exit and scurries in the opposite direction.

Chuckling, I don't bother grabbing my coat to make it look less noticeable and pause in the doorway, waiting for her. Something hanging above catches my attention, and it's like a beacon telling me that what is about to happen tonight will change everything. Despite not being in Norway, this *Jul* will surpass them all. Draping from the doorway is a clump of green leaves and plastic tiny, white berries tied together with red ribbon.

Mistletoe.

FIFTEEN

THEODORA

I'M BESIDE MYSELF. Here I am, counting to one hundred and twenty seconds in my head knowingly, whisking away soon to spend a *night* with Axel in ways I can't imagine when I thought the worst of him moments earlier. But he turns out to be nothing like my ex and the polar opposite of him. He didn't seek to remove *me* from the byline but *himself* on my behalf. What parallel universe have I stepped into, and who do I talk to about a lifelong subscription?

I get to sixty-two seconds and can't take it anymore. If I don't have Axel's hands on me stat, I may seriously combust. And this would be a real downer for anyone nearby. So, in theory, I'm having sex with Axel for the betterment of the world—for holiday spirit.

I'm throwing my coat on a beat later, rummaging through my notebooks, and grabbing my doodling and note-taking ones.

"Ditching us, are you?" Rupert asks, his voice suddenly posh and borderline British for whatever reason.

Desiree appears at his side, an all too knowing smug grin on her face, lips locked to her cup of punch.

"Not ditching. I had an epiphany for the story, and want to get it all written out before it escapes me. You *both* know how that is." I shove the notebooks in my bag and toss the strap over one shoulder.

"Why don't you jot notes while you're here?" Desiree's cup flails around the office, that coy smile still plastered to her big fat mouth.

"Are you kidding?" I snort and lean on my desk chair, stumbling when it rolls away from me. "It's far too distracting here. The music, the lights, the overlapping conversations. I'd barely get a sentence out, let alone paragraphs."

They look at me incredulously after swapping "She's so getting a lump of coal from Santa this year," glances at each other.

A tingle settles over my skin, knowing Axel waits for me right outside, and I'm about to have one of the best nights of my life. It's a preconceived declaration, I know, but I can't deny the swoop he gives my stomach whenever I'm near him—the way I can feel my face light up when he catches my gaze, or the laugh only he can seem to pull from me—the one reserved in a bottomless pit of my stomach.

"Anyway, duty calls." I give them a pageant wave and turn on my heel.

"More like booty calls," Rupert mumbles to Desiree, giggling.

The sound of Desiree's hand swatting his shoulder and Rupert shrieking a girl-like "ouch" makes me pause and finally look at them.

Rupert pretends to pout at Desiree and rubs his shoulder, but Desiree's eyes meet mine, and she mouths the words, "Have fun." It's all I need. And it's not as if I ask my friend's permission to sleep with whomever I please, but the sheer fact they're so in my corner about this makes my steps to the exit seem much lighter and effortless.

When I push through the double doors, Axel stands in the next doorway, casually leaning on the frame with his giant hands in his pockets. His legs cross at the ankles, and he points up with the most mischievous grin I've seen on him yet. There, hanging perfectly centered, thanks to Mary, is a sprig of mistletoe wrapped in bright red satin ribbon.

I take my time walking to him, exaggerating one foot crossing over the other until I, too, am nestled under the mistletoe with him. "Do Yule traditions have anything related to mistletoe?"

"Definitely." He sneaks a hand into my jacket, resting it on my hip. "It started back with the Celtic Druids. But the particular story I grew up with is the goddess Frigg being so happy the mistletoe saved Baldur's life that she vowed to kiss anyone who walked beneath some as a sign of love and appreciation."

Love and appreciation. These two words alone have my heart humming and my toes scrunching as much as they can scrunch within my shoes.

"Well, then—" I step forward and wrap my arms around his neck. "We shouldn't disappoint her."

His eyes go heavy, and he bends to me, pressing a soft kiss to my lips. He keeps it short. No more than three seconds because we both know this isn't the place for it. But the moment, this blissful holiday moment we share, can last two seconds or a hundred, and it'd still be perfection.

"Come on, Romance." Axel steps back and holds both hands out to me. "Time to start new traditions."

It's snowing outside the office—big chunky flakes that obscure your vision and are easy to catch on your tongue. The sidewalks have turned icy, and with the weather the way it is, they'll wait before throwing salt down. I yelp as my heels try mercilessly to gain traction, immediately regretting wearing them. But honestly, who wears a dress like this and snow boots? And though my mind made up all kinds of scenarios on what may or may not transpire tonight, walking to Axel's apartment to stay the night was not one of them. Otherwise, I would've prepared for it.

Axel chuckles and shakes stray snow from his beard before giving me his back. "Hop on."

I blink at him as if he asked me to pole vault onto his back versus a simple hop. "You're going to give me a piggy-back ride?"

"Why not?" He does a double take, eyes roaming my thighs, and nods. "Your coat's long enough to cover your ass." Axel hunches forward and pats his back. "I need you *not* broken tonight, and there's no way in hell you're going to make it in those shoes. So, Theodora—" He flashes me a stern yet playful stare over his shoulder. "Hop. On."

It's so incredibly twisted how turned on I get when he commands me but then again, this man could order me to have the last Oreo and I'd happily oblige. Because it's a game we play. We already have a "thing."

Calculating the trajectory from my height versus his and the distance from the ground, I jump and barely get myself over his butt. A hysterical laugh plummets from my gut—the special one he's risen from me—and I struggle not to fall off of him. He chuckles with me, his hands slide behind my knees and I'm secured on his back with one quick tug.

The sidewalks are unusually scarce of people. It's probably a good thing, considering Axel slips several times and steers us toward street lamps, newspaper dispensers, and vendor stalls to keep his balance with extra weight on his back. But he never drops me, falls, or sends us flying to our backs. When his beard gets loaded with snowflakes, I shake them out for him, and a permanent smile etches into my cheeks. Axel's grin only falters when he has to concentrate on not slipping, but otherwise, he's laughing and re-adjusting me on his back at every intersection.

We make it to Axel's apartment unscathed and with him serving as my gallant steed for the rest of the journey. We stand in the foyer in front of the elevators, and simultaneously reach for the up button making our hands brush.

Why couldn't *this* have been our meet cute? Not me being a total basket case and not holding the door for him?

The elevator ride lasts for only three floors, but we're a constant pattern of glances, curling pinky fingers, and brushing elbows. When the doors chime open, he leads me down the hall with yellow and royal blue ornate carpeting, and we stop in front of a white door with a gold number seventeen hanging over the peephole.

"Will you close your eyes for me?" Axel whispers against my cheek, jingling the keys in his pockets and readying them to unlock the door.

Heat pools in my cheeks and belly. Grinning, I do as he asks. The door opens and his hand rests on my lower back, guiding me into the apartment. My hands are outstretched in front of me, but he leads me well enough that my fingers never brush anything. I hear the door click shut and the deadbolt sliding into place and locking.

"Now you can look, Romance." I flutter my eyes open and let out a dreamy gasp, my hands flying to my gaping mouth.

A spruce tree rests in the center, a wall of windows displaying the Chicago skyline behind it. Simple decorations adorn the tree: berries, warm white lights, and pinecones. Axel steps to a fireplace on the right-side wall and lights it, the dancing orange flames spilling dancing fairy shadows across the room. The same spruce branches, berries, and white lights decorate the fireplace's mantle, and two stockings hang on opposite ends—one dark blue, the other light. Paper stars with tiny holes and glowing warm white light inside dangle from every corner. A single log with markings carved into it is the only thing nestled under the tree.

"Axel, this is so—" I'm getting teary-eyed, and can scarcely believe it. "—perfect."

A smile edges Axel's lips, but this one is different—bashful even. He motions for me to come to him. "It's only right if you do this with me." He picks up the log from under the tree and tosses it in his palms.

"What is this?" I drag my fingertips over the markings.

"This is our *Jul* log. The markings represent things you hope for in the coming year. We toss the log into the fire and let it burn through the night until the sun rises."

I'm still mesmerized by the carvings and cant my head as if I could somehow decipher them. "And what do these mean?"

He points to each symbol as he describes them. "Strength, prosperity, and growth. Did you want anything else added before we toss it in?"

I nibble my bottom lip. "Is there one for joy?"

"Yes." His smile is sugarplums and steaming cocoa and has me so jittery to get my hands on him that I can scarcely stand it. He carves another symbol into the log, a straight line with a triangular shape at the top, resembling a jagged "p." "This rune can also mean *ecstasy* depending on how you interpret it."

His lips gently brush mine and my stomach swoops to the Earth's core. Together, we toss the log into the fire, this one sparking brighter than the rest, blue flames spurt from underneath it until settling into orange and yellow with the rest.

"And now, we wait to watch the sunrise." Axel rubs a hand up and down my back like it's something he's done a thousand times. The familiarity of it has my insides warming along with the fire heating my skin.

"You had no qualms with trying to give me the romance piece all to myself because you can't write fiction, let alone romance, can you?" My brow gives a playful bob, gaze still fixating on the bouncing flames and orange embers.

His palm stills between my shoulder blades. "I never said I *couldn't* write fiction. I've never tried."

"Mmhm. Yup." I turn for my bag and pull out the jotting notebook and a pen. "I don't think you can."

A flippant chuckle escapes Axel's throat, and he's scratching the back of his shaved head. "Is this you getting back at me for going behind your back to Simone?"

"Maybe." I drag out the "a" and flip to a fresh piece of paper after resting my butt on the edge of his glossy, mahogany desk. For some reason, I lick the tip of my pen like a quill and sputter when the taste of ink coats my tongue.

"What are you doing?"

I scribble something, but it's drivel. Random words and phrases to keep the pen moving. "Taking notes. Had a few ideas for the story pop into my head."

"Uh-huh." Axel folds those burly arms and backs away in one, two, three strides. "Alright, Romance. How's this?"

What is he doing?

"A Viking and a Shieldmaiden—partnered for several summers now, met in the heat of battle and the battlefield is where they've remained." He takes a single step forward and mimics gestures like a sword is in his grasp.

I clutch the corner of my notebook, wincing as one of the wire coils of binding has gone rogue and pokes itself against my skin.

"They raid together. Protect their clan together."

Damn the wire. It can puncture my skin now for all I care.

He takes another step closer. "But the battle they fought today? It was unlike any other. They almost took their journey to Valhalla and would've been happy to do so."

My chest pulses up and down, and breathing becomes an erratic nuisance.

"But the universe still has plans for them. And to celebrate their lives together, the opportunity to still give the world *something*—" Axel looms over me now, his finger trailing up my exposed calf, making me shiver. "—the Viking leads the Shieldmaiden to his furs in the longhouse and tells her—" He plucks the pen from my loose grip, tossing it to the side. "—time to lay down sword and shield—" He peels the notebook from my chest with nimble fingers and tosses it on the marble kitchen island. "For tonight, instead of cries of victory—" His hands slip between my knees, gently coaxing them apart. "—it'll be *roars* of pleasure."

I'm a complete and utter mess. I can't remember my own name, let alone what planet we're on.

Axel's lips hover near mine, and suddenly, he's smiling. "How'd I do?"

"I—" Nope. Still a mess. My mouth gapes and all I can do is sway. His thighs are between my legs, my center brushing his jeans, and only the thin lace of my underwear separates us. "—I retract my statement?"

His hand raises to press against the wall near my head. "That day I caught you daydreaming? What were you honestly thinking about?"

There's no sense in hiding it. Especially not after this display. I mean, holy hell.

"You Axel. I was thinking about *you*."

A low, rumbly growl bubbles in his throat, and as his eyelids grow heavy, it darkens his gaze. "Tell me."

As much as I don't want to move from where we are, a small part of me hopes he wants to reenact it.

I push a hand to his chest, and he slides backward, letting me move away from the desk. "Not surprisingly, you were a Viking and had just returned from battle to visit my tent."

His hands clench at his sides like he's about to pounce me at any moment, and the thought has that spot between my legs *pulsing*. "And why would I be visiting your tent?"

Gulping, I play with the hem of my green dress. "I was yours, and you wished to settle the—frenzy—with me."

Veins bulge in his arms now, giving the tattoo edges and shadows. "Did we bother taking off our clothes?"

No sooner do I shake my head than his hands are on my hips, lifting me from the ground and storming us back to the desk. His mouth crashes to mine, our tongues melding, teeth occasionally clattering from the sheer chaos of this kiss. He rests my butt on the desk, the coolness shocking at first, enough to make me gasp, but the infernal heat coursing through me soon douses it.

He's undoing his belt, one hand flicking it open while the other tangles in my hair, and he keeps kissing me. The sound of the zipper going down has my heart catapulting into a furious gallop, and when his hand leaves my head to join the other in bunching my dress at my hips, I damn near lose all sense of control.

His hardness is on full display now, and it doesn't disappoint. Its sheer size should make me feel hesitant or reserved, but I just don't care. It could be a tantalizing mix of short-lived pain mixed with pleasure until the ecstasy took over, and I wouldn't *care*. Callused fingers trail my folds as he peels my underwear to one side. A single finger slips in, and this alone has my back arching. He adds another finger, probing in and out of me, and I whimper.

"Damn, Theo," he gruffly whispers against my temple.

He's undoubtedly talking about the torrential downpour I've become over him.

"You going to work out the frenzy, Viking?" I catch his gaze, my nails scraping the back of his skull. "Or *talk* about it?"

At this, he grabs both calves and pulls me forward until I'm balancing on the desk's edge. Our gazes are locked but the sound of him tearing the foil packet open, his knuckles brushing my inner thighs as he works it over his shaft has me panting. My eyes focus on his forearm flexing, but when the hardened tip pushes into my entrance, the dim lighting in the room makes me see stars. He pauses only long enough for me to flutter back to reality before driving the rest of the way in. I cry out, not caring that I forgot to ask about neighbors. With one hand on the wall behind me for leverage, he thrusts over and over, my skin squeaking against the gloss desk, wood pounding against the wall with every pump.

I keep one hand gripping for dear life on the desk and the other curls behind Axel's neck, using my strength to pound against him every time he comes forward. Our bodies slap together in glorious unison, the tightening, pleasuring ache forming in my core. Tilting my chin to the ceiling, I let it consume me and moan through my climax, tightening around him and making him grunt against my neck.

He dives into another round of conquering thrusts and pounds and he's holding onto both butt cheeks now, ramming into me with the ferocity of a damn bear. I cry out again and he joins me this time, coming undone, stilling, twitching, and soon boneless and leaning over me on the desk.

"Was that my *Jul* gift?" I ask, playfully sliding my foot up the back of his leg.

A sheen of sweat coats his bronzed skin, his breaths shorter but not near breathless. "I've not even *begun* to gift you, Romance."

He cradles me in his arms, and carries me to the plush chocolate couch resting between the tree and a glass coffee table. He tosses me onto it but doesn't join me straight away, giving his back to me as he tosses something away. I sit up on my elbows and greedily bite my bottom lip. The desperation to see Axel fully naked is an ache carving into my bones. How elaborate is that tattoo?

As if reading my mind, he faces me and peels the shirt away first. The tattoo goes up his bicep, over his shoulder, and continues to his pec but stops just above the nipple. When he turns to take off his boots, I spy the tattoo coursing over most of his upper back on that same side, too. His jeans are off in one sweep.

I laugh at the site of metallic red boxers. "You weren't lying."

"Theo—" He turns to face me, gripping the boxers and dragging them down. "—one thing you need to know about me—" Axel's on top of me now, pressing a knee into the couch cushion beneath me, and my hands are already ravenously moving toward the two mounds of muscular flesh that make up his perfect ass. "—*I'm no liar.*"

And I believe him. I truly do.

He helps me out of my dress and makes torturous work of slipping my panties down my legs, grazing his teeth over my thigh, knee, and calf. When he returns, he holds himself above me with one arm gripping the couch's back, the other firmly placed by my head. He's between my thighs, and this time, when he pushes into me, it's slow and sweet and languid. We take our time with this one because we have all night to explore every inch of each other. And in this one instance, I wish the sun would never rise.

SIXTEEN

AXEL

THE WOMAN IN my arms is nothing short of amazing. She's creative, talented, beautiful, insatiable, and I have her all to myself. And sex with her? It's beyond anything I conjured in my brain the several times I imagined *her* while taking care of myself. We've only been in my place for two hours and have already christened my desk, the couch, the kitchen counter, and the floor we now lie on. Ironically, we're sprawled on the puffy comforter from my bed, but have yet actually to *use* said bed. I'd yanked the blanket draped over my couch to cover us, curling Theo to my side and positioning us next to the tree.

Unfortunately, my tree stands too close to the ground for us to fit under it, but she's still mesmerized by it all the same. I kiss the top of her head, making lazy strokes up and down her arm with my fingers. The soothing old Norse melodies of my favorite band *Wardruna* lightly play in the background. "I'd like to ask you something, Theo, but you don't have to answer me if you don't want to."

She lets out a blissful sigh before turning to face me, her breasts pushing against my chest. "Is it something to do with why I insisted on avoiding you? Why didn't I just come out and tell you what I'd overheard?"

I swear this woman *can* read minds.

Nodding, I let my gaze follow her body's curves—the roundness of her shoulder, the dip that forms from her ribs to her hip, and the smooth, taut line down the apex of her thigh.

"My ex. The paper I worked for before Celestial Magazine, well, he was my co-worker." Theo pauses, her eyes pinching shut, and her fingers tap my sternum bone.

I can see where this story's going before it's ended and feel that much more of an ass. The knowledge that I triggered this fear in her by going behind her back to talk to Simone has guilt spiraling through me like a blizzard. "Theo, you don't have to tell me."

"No. I want to. I do." Her eyes blast open, and she busies herself by tracing the patterns in my tattoo. "I was assigned a project he wanted, and despite the two years we'd spent together, he let his resentment and jealousy get the better of him."

I trail a hand to her head, using my fingers to knead her scalp.

"Not only did he steal my story but announced in front of the entire company that *he* was the one who'd written it and him alone." Theo's petite hand curls into a fist against my chest.

"I'm so sorry, Theo. I had no idea." A frown pulls at my lips, and I pinch her chin, hoping her eyes would lift to mine. They do.

"How could you have known?" One pale shoulder shrugs, and a fluttery short chuckle follows. "I'm sorry I avoided you. I should've immediately approached you about it, but I felt bad for eavesdropping and ashamed of how quickly I feared the worst all because of one freaking man from my past."

The fireplace crackles, and the orange glint from the flames shadows her skin.

"You don't need to apologize for being vulnerable, Theo. And as much as we'd all love to think our pasts don't define us, particularly those times we've been hurt, it's a damn lie." I press a soft kiss on her forehead. "Do you want your first *Jul* gift?"

Her head perks up at this. "First? How many are there?"

"Twelve. One for each day."

Theo scoots closer to me, her hand exploring my stomach. The feather-like touches make goosebumps scatter across my skin, and my length grows hard *again*. "Growing up did you only open one present on the twenty-fifth?"

"Nah, we did the whole eve and day of craziness of opening dozens of presents, too. But there was also always one really special gift for *Jul*." Reaching past her, I remove the small goat ornament from a branch and hand it to her. "Happy *Jul*, Theo." I kiss the tip of her nose.

Her emerald eyes light up as she takes the goat. "This is adorable. Did you make it?"

"Yeah," I admit. And it hadn't been easy. It's been years since I built a *Jul* goat from scratch using straw, and the ones I made in the past were triple this size.

"Shut up. Really?" Theo sits up and holds the goat to the light bouncing from the fire. "Thanks so much, Ax. This means the world to me. But also—" Playfully, she swats me on the shoulder, and my gaze darts to how her bare breasts bounce.

"Ouch," I say through a laugh, rubbing my arm like it hurt. "What was that for?"

"You didn't tell me we were exchanging presents." She sticks her bottom lip out in an exaggerated pout. "Wait." Theo leaps to her feet, and, wearing nothing but a smile, she walks to her bag resting on the kitchen counter. After rummaging through it, she yanks a yellow notebook, rips out a page, quickly scribbles something on it, and returns, handing me a piece of paper.

I arch a quizzical brow and take it, snickering at the Viking cartoon I'd caught her doodling days prior.

"You were right. It *is* you." Theo sits on her heels beside me, curling the blanket halfway around herself.

It's the drawing, but now the words: "To Axel" are written in one corner, and "From: Theo Happy Yule" in the other corner.

"Thank you, sweetheart. I'll have to get this framed and hang it by my desk." I wink at her, and she bounces, tormenting me with her bouncing breasts again before she gives me her back and scoots her ass as close as she can against my hips.

She's staring at the tree now, her wandering eyes moving from the top branches and pausing in the middle, where she cocks her head to one side. "That Santa ornament." She points. "His clothes and everything look a little different. Is that supposed to be a Father Christmas depiction or something? He's not even wearing red."

Leaning over her, I pluck the ornament off the tree and hold it in front of her, running my thumb over the carved wood—a man with long white hair and beard, sporting a blue-hooded cloak with white fur trim. "That's because this isn't Santa. It's Odin."

"Odin?" She traces a finger over the figure's face.

"The story is that during this time of year, Odin would travel to earth on his, and I know this sounds weird, but, eight-legged horse—"

Theo grabs my arm and interrupts with, "Wait. Eight? Like how there's eight reindeer?"

"Caught onto that, did you?" I chuckle and brush a stray strand of hair from her face. "Yes. But he would visit the people to check on how they were doing, remaining invisible to them, and leave bread for those that needed it." Kissing her cheek, I wrap my arms around her tighter. "Children would leave their shoes by the hearth the night before the winter solstice with sugar and hay for Odin's horse. And at those homes, he'd leave a toy or candy."

Theo takes the ornament into her hand. "I'm so blown away by all of this."

"And if you notice—" I point to the figure missing its left eye. "That's how you can also tell it's not Santa."

"And does that have a story to accompany it, too?" Theo tilts her head back to look at me, her hand trailing down the length of my tattoo, starting at the shoulder. "And this?"

"There are many, many stories, Romance. And I'll tell you any you want to hear." I lightly bump her cheek with a knuckle.

Theo gasps and snaps her fingers. "Speaking of story. I think I just got an idea for the ending of the holiday hockey romance. A *grand* gesture."

"Grand gesture?" I ask, but she's already catapulting to her feet after handing me the ornament and scurrying to her bag.

She returns with an iPad and flops to the floor atop the comforter, leaning her back on the couch. "Yes. In a lot of romance stories, it's like this elaborate display of affection without using verbal communication."

I shift positions so I'm leaning on an elbow beside her, watching her fingers fly over the touchscreen keyboard. "Gotcha. I assume the hero will be making said gesture?"

"The *hero*." She bumps her shoulder against mine, snorting. "You learn so fast. But no. In this one, I'm making the heroine do it."

"You rebel, you." Of their own volition, my fingers trace circles around her knee.

She pauses typing and gives me a warm, inviting smile. "I personally believe women shouldn't expect dudes to go out of their way to show someone they love them all the time. Us gals must take the reins occasionally, too, you know?"

The skin below one of my eyes twitches. "Is this a loaded question?"

Fortunately, she does me the courtesy of not making me answer and giggles before tapping a finger against her lip. "Hm. Do I go with a scavenger hunt or a flash mob?"

I've lost count of the new words, concepts, and phrases I've learned since meeting Theodora Hackett. This adds to the ever-growing list.

"Flash mob?"

She drops her hand, the tablet falling with it, and she gasps. "You've never heard of a flash mob?"

Looking from the tree, to the fireplace, then back to her face, I shake my head.

"Oh, my—" She sits cross-legged and rests the tablet between us before securing her hair over her ears.

I'm in awe of how easily she has a normal conversation in the buff with me, and I'm not complaining about it one bit.

"So, it's this choreographed number that's either singing or dancing or both. Then you have everyone dress normal, blend in with the crowd, plan it for somewhere you know they'll be, and then suddenly they break into this routine around said person." She does jazz hands, palms facing me, and shaking them. "Neat, huh?"

"Sounds—" I scratch the back of my head, careful to tread lightly on my next words. "—elaborate?"

"Most grand gestures are. They don't have to be, but," The iPad is back in her grasp. "Think I should go with the scavenger hunt?"

"I think it would make it more personable. It could be a roadmap of key milestones throughout their relationship." I gaze at the windows, eyeing the dark skies and dim stars—so much light in the city. Norway's skies have so many stars in unending patches it looks like the gathering of freckles on Theo's shoulders.

"I love that idea. See?" Theo's face appears in mine, and she kisses me, soft and sweet. "This is why I wouldn't feel right not having you on that byline with me, Ax."

"Thank you for that, by the way." I touch one corner of her jaw and drag my finger to the other side. "You hungry?"

"I am actually. Burnt a lot of calories the past few hours." Lust plays in her gaze, and she nibbles her lower lip.

"In that case—" I stand, letting the blanket fall to the floor, and watch her gaze fall straight to my crotch. "—I better fuel you up. Because the night is young, Romance. And I'm not nearly done *ravishing* you."

Theo gulps as she pans her eyes up my stomach and lands on my face. She scrapes her nails over her throat as I pass her, and I can feel her burning stare on my ass. Chuckling to myself, wondering how I've suddenly become such a lucky bastard, I grab the bag of chestnuts from my cupboard, a bottle of red wine, and two glasses. The goods now loaded in my hands, I return to find her typing away on the iPad again, a concentrated wrinkle forming on her forehead. I don't dare interrupt her and watch from afar, grinning at how the tip of her tongue ever so slightly sticks from the corner of her mouth, her right foot bounces, and she doesn't blink. Not once.

"Has anyone ever told you it's incredibly hot to watch you

work?" I squat by the fire, resting everything in an organized pile.

"And the fact I'm naked doesn't help at all, right?" Theo flashes me a sultry smile, taps a few more times on the iPad, and then it's off and tossed behind her onto the couch.

I'm still squatting and resting my elbows on my thighs, grinning back at her. "Oh, it definitely does."

She crawls toward me on her hands and knees like a tigress approaching her mate. Her lips are on mine, tongue teasing the seam of my mouth. "You really don't lie, do you?"

I slip a hand to the back of her neck and rub our noses together. "My nose gets bigger if I do."

"Nose, huh? I figured it'd be Axel Junior that gave you away." Her eyes drop to the hard-on I got from watching her crawl toward me like that.

I suck in a breath and cup her face with my palms. "He never *ever* lies."

"We certainly shouldn't keep him waiting." She smiles against my mouth. Her fingers trail down my length, pulling a strangled snarl from the pit of my stomach.

A breath later, she's cradled in my arms like I had her in the snow by the lake, and we're on my bed. As the night dwindles, we roast chestnuts, get tipsy on wine, and screw like rabbits another two times. We're sitting on my couch, staring at the tree and silent in each other's arms, with the blanket covering us. The fire has started to die, and the *Jul* log has almost burnt to ash. Her knees curl over my lap, and her head rests on my shoulder with a contented sigh. She drifts to sleep, the steady sounds of her deep, slumbering breaths almost lulling me to dreamland as well, but I force my eyes to stay open, knowing sunrise is at any moment.

When the sky turns dull shades of dark blue with slivers of yellow and orange, I gently shake Theo awake. Groggily, she smacks her lips together and rubs the heel of her palm against her eye. "Did I fall asleep? Did I miss it?"

"You didn't miss it. Look." I nudge my chin at the windows as the sun peeks over the horizon.

All tiredness falls away from her, and she sits up straight, marveling at the natural light art the sun provides. Purply hues mixed with a fiery red spill across the sky nestled between two skyscrapers.

Theo wraps her arms around one of mine, nuzzling against me and resting her head on my shoulder. "Happy *Jul*, my Viking."

A tightness forms in my chest over the depths I've managed to fall for this woman. I'm falling, plummeting, with no desire to reach the ground because I'm perfectly content with making her my whole world if she lets me.

"Happy *Jul*, Romance." I nestle my head atop hers, and as the sun fully blazes the Chicago skyline, we fall asleep in a cozy embrace.

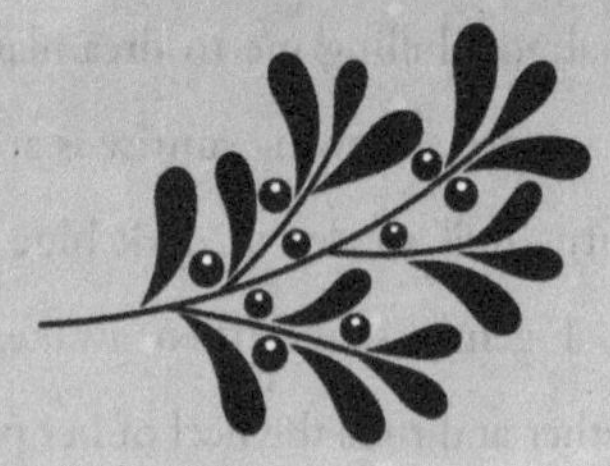

SEVENTEEN

THEODORA

THE PAST TWENTY-FOUR hours feel akin to a fever dream. I've lived through the moments, have experienced the sights, and smells, and *felt* everything. But such euphoria and blissful happiness seem imaginary somehow. We fell asleep no sooner had the sun risen, having stayed awake all night, and I'm the first to wake at one o'clock in the afternoon. When my eyes flutter open, finding Axel still fast asleep, I don't make a sound or dare to move because I want to watch him. And not in some creepy way, I just enjoy seeing him in this intimate, vulnerable state.

His breaths are deep and slowed, his arm resting comfortably around my shoulders. His lips are slightly parted, and a dull snore escapes from his throat, his head turned at an odd angle from the couch. He looks so peaceful, so serene—a stark contrast to the tall, hulky, Viking persona I'd given him. When he stirs, I let my eyes fall shut, pretending I'm still asleep.

He grumbles but stills suddenly as if he doesn't want to wake me. I save him the trouble by lazily opening my eyes and cooing against his side. "What time is it?"

"After one," Axel answers, his voice gravelly when he first awakes, and the deeper pitch of it has my insides collapsing over each other.

"I guess that's what happens when you stay up until six in the morning, hm?" Chuckling, I dip my hand under the blanket, seeking the warmth of his bare chest, humming when I find it.

Axel groans and rubs his eyes with one hand, stifling a yawn. "I know you don't want to hear this right now, but we need to wrap up the stories. Simone said she needs it in hand by the end of business *today*, which is in four hours."

I join in his mumbles of groans before I dramatically flop to my back on the couch cushion. "I really don't want to go into the office today."

"We don't have to." Axel appears over me, caging me in with his burly Scandinavian arms and smiles. "I can grab my laptop, and we can access the shared drive from it. Submit the finished product right from this couch and still naked as the day we were born."

Axel's beard has become unkempt from our escapades and sleep, so I comb my fingers through it. "Do you have coffee?"

"I *am* a writer." He does a sort of snorting chuckle and traces a thumb over one of my eyebrows.

"Where is everything? I'll start a pot while you set up stuff on your laptop."

He rubs my nose with his. "Grains are in the top left cabinet. Mugs are in the cabinet right below it. Sugar is next to the maker."

"Creamer?"

Axel winces and rakes two fingers through my hair, pausing when he snags on a tiny knot that's formed, smoothing it out. "Sorry. I usually only do sugar. There's milk, though."

"Perfect." I give him a reassuring smile.

After a deep sigh, Axel crawls off me and stands, stretching his arms above him. That hardness I've felt countless times inside me is there in all its morning glory as his back arches and he groggily scratches the back of his head. The product he uses to keep his hair slicked back has given up and shambles of blonde locks fall over his gaze.

"You keep looking at me like that, Romance, and we're going to miss our deadline." A devilish grin plays on his lips, his finger pointing at my face.

I'm unsure at what point my gaze turned into starving with lust and my hand found its way to my breasts, but I fan a palm over my face, turning it back to neutral as best I can. Because as much as I want to say screw the deadline, you *don't* screw with Simone. And this was both our jobs on the line.

"You're right. We have plenty of time for hanky panky after we turn in the stories." I clap my hands together and leap to my feet. The chill in the air has me fumbling for the blanket to wrap myself in, the fire now only glowing embers in the hearth.

"Hanky panky," Axel mumbles as he makes his way down the hall, shaking his head and chuckling.

I bite my thumbnail as I watch his perfectly toned butt walk away—*flex, bounce, flex, bounce.*

Axel points toward the kitchen before disappearing into another room. "Coffee, Theo."

"Right," I shout, hurrying to the kitchen and doing as I said I would.

Moments later, we're on the couch again, laptop open and ready on the table in front of us. We consume three pots of coffee, bouncing ideas back and forth and revising as we go. Axel finishes his article within thirty minutes, I proofread it, and approximately three hours later, we have two polished and ready-to-publish pieces of work to submit. I throw my legs over his lap, smiling at him after planting a satisfied kiss against his lips. And together, we tap our forefingers to the touchpad, submitting it.

Axel pats my thigh. "Let's get dressed. It's almost time for your next *Jul* gift."

"It's not here?" I ask, confused, and point at the floorboards like he's hidden it there.

Gently, Axel moves my legs from over him and coaxes me to stand. "No. And you're welcome to use the shower and everything if you'd like."

"Or—" I saunter closer and finger walk up his taut, tanned chest. "We could both take a shower and save time?"

"Don't have to ask me twice." Axel's gaze turns downright

feral and I'm on my stomach on his shoulder, butt in the air in a fireman's carry.

Shrieking and laughing as Axel carries me down the hallway, I take the opportunity to swat his bare ass, and he does the same right back to me. After sudsing each other up and making love again with my back slammed against the tiled wall, we've blow-dried our hair, dressed, and I beg him to stop by my apartment so I can grab something warmer to wear and slap on more make-up.

He's pacing my living room while I'm in the bedroom, rummaging through my closet. And it's gone far too quiet out there for comfort. "You alright out there?" I call out.

"Yeah, I'm just gawking at your decorations or lack thereof. I thought you'd have a bigger tree. And more—well—everything."

Admittedly, I didn't decorate my apartment this year as much as I usually do, which made the sight of Axel's apartment when I opened my eyes that much more magical. I settle on a pair of light skinny jeans, a dark blue sweater, and tan boots, which I hop on one foot down the hall as I slide them on. "I've never had as big a tree as yours because my apartment is half the size of yours, Ax. And as far as the decorations? I hadn't felt much in the spirit this year." I frown at the one strip of garland hanging from my kitchen island and cheesy static clings in the front window.

"And now?" Axel chuckles at the sight of me still hopping around and moves beside me so I can use him to balance.

Finally wedging my heel in the boot, I let it flop to the floor, and stand straight, throwing my arms around his neck. "I'm at a level I wasn't sure I could get anymore. And I have you to thank for that. Have *Jul* to thank for that."

Grinning, his arms are around my waist, and he gives a quick peck to my lips. "Good. Now grab your coat." He pats my butt twice. "We're going to be late."

"Late?" Doing as he asks, I throw my jacket over my shoulders and snatch my scarf. "Where are we going?"

"Do you always ask this many questions when someone's trying to surprise you?" His light brows raise, and he moves to the door, holding it open for me.

Surrendering, I hold my palms up. "Alright, alright. Surprise away."

Curiosity and anticipation continue to plague my brain as we walk through the streets of downtown. It's not until we arrive at the train station that the thought dawns on what exactly he may have arranged. Tears form in my eyes when the familiar red and green train rolls to a stop in front of us, the lights bordering each window.

"Did you book us on the holiday train, Ax?" I affectionately slap him with my glove.

He grins and kisses my cheek after pulling me to his side. "Yes, I did. Ready to board the Polar Express?"

Laughing and jumping, I hold his hand and enter the train filled to the brim with other passengers seeking holiday cheer so close to Christmas. We find our assigned seats, and I'm so excited I can't seem to find it in me to sit back. I'm wringing my hands on the railing and turning every which way, wondering who or what will happen next. I'm like a kid again, and the train may as well be freaking Disney World.

The workers dressed as elves come through the train with candy and small boxes wrapped in green and red foil wrapping paper. Each box has a Chicago keychain or magnet inside. And though they more than likely cost a buck a piece, the sentiment is adorable, and I know I'll cherish mine for years to come. We sing *Jingle Bells, Santa Claus is Coming to Town*, and *Let it Snow*, all the while zipping through a circular tour of the city, the lights within the car timed to the beat of the music.

When the ride pulls to a stop, they advise us that Santa will be waiting for anyone who wants to meet him, and the small children in our car scream with delight. We're on the approach now, and I tackle Ax, him catching me with those muscular arms just below my butt cheeks. I hold his face with both hands and kiss him, the faint sounds of holiday music still hanging in the air from the train.

"*Takk*," I whisper.

Axel peels back, surprised. "Did you just speak Norwegian?"

"I think you mean *Norsk*." I chew on my lip, happily still suspended in the air.

"You—are you—" Axel doesn't know what to say, and the bewilderment in his intense eyes has me reeling.

"I started learning on Duolingo. That's my second *Jul* gift, Ax."

Axel's eyes take on a gentleness and awe that I've yet to see. "*Du er en skatt.*"

Blinking, not knowing what he said aside from some form of

"you are," I tap the back of his neck. "I'm only on unit two, Ax."

A roaring chuckle thunders from his chest, and with me still in his arms, he trots down the approach.

The next day is Christmas Eve, and we're all begrudgingly in the office. Axel and I, most of all, look like we've just been told zombies are real and stampeding through lower Whacker Drive. We try everything not to look at each other longingly and don't dare to be in the same vicinity because all we want to do is hold hands, kiss, or touch a part of us to something of the other. It's ridiculous as much as it is romantic, and I decide I cannot and will never be able to get enough of this man.

"So," Desiree croons, dragging out the "o" and leaning a hip on my desk. "How was *your* weekend?"

Rupert appears next, leaning on his forearms in front of me. "And leave no stone unturned."

A glance at Axel, who is already eyeballing these two knuckleheads, has me biting back a smile. "It was a very relaxing, thought-provoking weekend. Thank you. And how was yours?"

"Oh, you're no fun," Rupert scoffs and pushes from the desk.

Desiree snickers and brushes my hair over one shoulder. "You're so full of shit. Your skin is flushed just thinking about your *relaxed* weekend, and your posture is so lackadaisical it's almost melting *me* into the floor."

I steal another look at Axel, and Rupert points in my face. "Ah ha. I would've been so miffed if we covered for you with Simone, and you didn't even get la—"

Simone storms from her office, cutting Rupert's sentence. "Everyone, gather around, we're having a staff meeting. *Now*."

The tone in her voice has my throat tightening. Had our stories inexplicably sucked? Did she wait all that time, poured all her resources into it, for absolutely nothing?

Gulping, I stand, and Axel is beside me within two strides. We stand near each other but not so close as to make it seem like we're *together*. But I can't help my body's constant instinct to lean toward him.

"As you all know, the special holiday e-magazine posted this morning," Simone starts, holding a stapled packet of papers in her hand that she shoves under one arm as she talks. "And I have to say, I've never seen numbers like this in such a short time."

Numbers? High numbers? Low numbers? The anticipation is killing me and all I want is to grab Axel's hand and hold onto it for dear life.

"We've broken a record, and we have these two to thank for it." Simone nudges her head at me and Axel.

The words don't register immediately, and it doesn't fully dawn on me until Axel's hands are on my shoulders, jostling me. "Did you hear that, Romance? Our pieces are a *hit*."

"Really?" I whisper, gleaming up at him.

"There was a reason I waited until the last minute to assign you the holiday story this year, Romance." Simone folds her arms, chin raising with pride. "I wanted this to feel real. For you to pull from authentic experiences."

My fingers grow tingly and a tic bounces in my cheek. Where is she going with this?

"This has gone over so well in fact—" Simone appears in front of us and slaps down the papers with so many numbers on them they all blend as I stare at them. "I'm making you two permanent partners. I figure we'll do these quarterly and publish them collected at the end of each year starting next year as a physical holiday anthology special."

"Pretty sure they're already *permanent* partners," Rupert says behind us, whistling.

Axel clears his throat and coughs into his fist. "I—ma'am—don't know what to say. Thank you."

"No thanks necessary. They were fabulous combined pieces, and readers became feral for it." Simone flicks something from her nail, looking between us as if waiting for us to say or do something.

Was she waiting for my gratitude as well?

"Um, yes. Thank you, Simone. It was an enjoyable piece to work on, and I can't wait to write more with Axel." I tap my fingers together behind my back.

"Something you two want to tell me?" Simone's expression borders on impatience mixed with a complete lack of enthusiasm.

Axel looks around us as if the answer lies somewhere within the sea of cubicles. "I'm sorry?"

"Look—" Simone sighs, closes the distance between us, now standing toe-to-toe. "—I have no policy against dating within the workplace, but just do me a favor?" She lowers her face and raises a silver-tipped pointy fingernail. "No more late-night office rendezvous? There *are* cameras in here." Nonchalantly, she moves her finger to each office corner.

My entire body flushes with heat, and I force a laugh. "Yes. Yes, ma'am. Sorry, ma'am."

Axel's hand finds my lower back, and he rubs it. "It won't happen again, boss."

Did she knowingly set us up? This doesn't seem like her.

"Simone, did you play match-maker?" My hands are a flighty mess when I ask this.

Simone scrunches her nose. "God, no. That was an unintended bonus."

"I—" Axel starts, scratching the back of his neck. "Thank—you?"

Simone taps the stack of papers before turning on her heel and heading back to her office. "Oh, and everyone, to celebrate this milestone, I'm giving you all the rest of the week off. Enjoy your holiday."

And Simone's heart grew three times this day.

Whoops and cheers burst through the office, and the floor becomes chaotic, with chairs being rolled to desks, jackets being grabbed, and computers shutting down. Everyone moves with urgency as if Simone would reappear and take it back.

"So, Axel, have any brooding Viking brothers by chance?"

Desiree asks, sidling beside us with her arms folded.

Axel laughs, his bright blue eyes glistening. "A much younger brother, but he lives in Norway, I'm afraid. However, I do have a lawyer friend."

Desiree snaps her gaze to me, her hands dropping at her sides before looking back to Axel. "What kind of lawyer?"

Axel nudges me with his elbow. "Criminal prosecutor."

"He's married, isn't he?" Rupert chimes in.

"No, no. Very much single." Axel kisses my temple, and the action is so effortless that my heart springs into pirouettes.

"Don't you have all the luck?" Rupert says, sticking his tongue out at Desiree.

Des narrows her eyes before pretending to grab his tongue. Rupert sucks it back in his mouth, and they both laugh.

"Anything in particular you want to do tomorrow, Romance?" Axel nuzzles into my neck, his breath coating my skin there.

"What would you normally do?"

"It's normally pretty relaxed with my family. We'd open some presents in the morning, eat a ham lunch-slash-dinner, nap, and see where the night takes us over warmed mugs of *gløgg*."

I close my eyes, imagining it all. "Sounds amazing. I want to do that. Just that." Peeking with one eye, I half-smile. "At your apartment. You're the one with the fireplace."

"Deal."

And I have my *own* grand gesture hidden up my sleeve for just such an occasion.

EIGHTEEN

AXEL

AFTER WE LEFT the office last night, we came home to my apartment, and I started a roaring fire. We sat on the couch and stared at it, talking about ourselves for hours. We shared a bottle of wine, roasted more chestnuts, and fell asleep on the couch. When I groggily awoke at two in the morning, I doused the fire and carried her to bed so we could get a good night's sleep for once.

Theo wakes me by pressing her soft lips against mine. She's peeling back the covers and crawling over me, her thighs straddling my hips. I smile up at her. The room is still dark save for the sliver of pale light creeping through the curtains. Her fingernails trail along my chest, and when she lowers herself onto me, the back of my head presses into the pillows from the sheer tightness of her, the slick, warm heat as she writhes on top of me.

We come undone together moments later, and she's nestled in

the crook of my arm, tracing patterns over my abs. If this was to be my next *Jul* gift, I can honestly say I've never had anything like it on the fifth day. And being it was her that gave it to me, I wouldn't have it any other way.

She jolts to her elbows and excitedly pats my shoulder. "Come on, you. Now it's *your* turn to get dressed and be ready for your next gift."

"This—" I widen my arms, signaling to our entwined naked bodies. "—wasn't it?"

She nibbles my arm, her gaze still playing on mine, and devilishly shakes her head. "No. I plan to give you this as often as possible. Wouldn't call that a gift."

"Trust me—" I cup her cheek, grazing my knuckles against her soft skin. "—it is."

Laughing, she pats my chest several times. "You can be so cheesy but don't ever, ever stop. Now get up. It's my turn to woo you."

I don't move at first, amused at her attempts to shove a body that weighs over a hundred pounds more than hers from the bed. Interlacing my hands behind my head, I watch her use only her hands at first, then resort to pushing my hips with her frigidly cold feet. The sudden contact makes me yelp, and I fan my palms in defeat.

"Okay, okay, so long as you keep those ice cubes away from my back." I chuckle and slide from under the covers, turning to spy her wiggling her toes at me and biting her lip.

She flips to her stomach to watch me walk down the hall, and I secretly hope she never stops looking at me that way. She's wearing the kind of expression that screams she wants to touch, devour, and consume me—a ravenous appetite that can never be truly satisfied, and she can't ever seem to get enough.

Keeping my promise, I grab my phone and dial Mom. She answers on the third ring and loud music blares in the background.

"*God Jul*, Axie," Mom yells, a slight slur in her voice suggesting she's on her third or fourth glass of *gløgg*.

Chuckling, I lean against the counter. "*God Jul, Mor*. Having a good time over there?"

"Oh, the best. Your brothers are wrestling and your sister is singing. Wish you were here."

"Me too, *Mor*. I'll let you get back to it. Have a good time. *Jeg elsker deg*."

Mom makes kissing sounds before hanging up and I smile, resting my phone on the kitchen island. But no sooner is it out of my hand, the phone chimes with an incoming text—a picture of Spencer with his mustache still intact, smiling, and holding a newspaper with today's date.

Faen.

Spencer: Time to pay up, buddy!

Sighing, I turn off the phone screen. "Hey Theo," I yell down the hall. "Hope you don't mind if I wear a Santa hat while we're out today."

After we're ready and properly caffeinated, we step into the hall of my apartment complex. I scratch my head through the red Santa hat snug against my skull. The cheap fabric itches my shaved sides. Theo is excitedly bouncing on her heels as I lock the door, and we're heading for the elevators. When one chimes open, Theo leaps in, pressing the button to *hold* it for me. Our gazes align as if we both have the same thought:

What would it have been like if she'd *held* the door for me that day?

Clearing my throat, I give her a curt nod but do a double take as if I'm seeing her for the first time. "Thanks for holding it for me, Miss—" I extend my hand to her, flashing a charming grin.

Theo eyes me sidelong, pretending not to ogle me, and shakes my hand. "Hackett. Theodora Hackett, but everyone calls me Theo."

I hold her hand longer than necessary, and the way I get lost in her eyes all over again isn't an act. "I'm Axel. You work in the building?"

Theo nibbles her bottom lip while still holding my hand. "I do. Celestial Magazine. Have you heard of it?"

Laughing, I reluctantly loosen my grip and our hands fall to our sides. "Heard of it? That's the magazine that recently hired me. Today's my first day."

"Shut up." She pretends like this is news to her and playfully swats my shoulder, pausing when she feels my bicep, and quickly looks away.

"I guess—" I start, turning to face her and slowly back her into the elevator wall. "—we'll be seeing a lot more of each other, hm?"

Theo's head slowly nods, her hands pressing to the metal behind her. I lower my face toward hers, our lips a breath apart, and the doors *bing*, opening to the lobby.

We smile at each other, and Theo jumps, planting a quick peck against my mouth. "As hot as that was and could have been, I still prefer not holding the door for you and you not knowing my name." She adjusts my hat and flicks the white poofy ball thing dangling by my cheek.

"Fair enough." I hook her arm with mine, and we exit. "It certainly seems to be more us. The other way almost seemed too easy. I firmly believe in working toward your happily ever after."

Theo tugs me, coaxing me to stop walking, and she's on her tippy toes, squishing my face between two gloved hands. "Man, do I lo—" She starts to say, her eyes widening in horror before she lets out a bout of nervous laughter and kisses me, never finishing her sentence.

Was she about to say what I think she was?

My heart throttles in my chest, and I choose to let it go for now. To not embarrass her further because I know the worth of saying those three words to someone. But the revelation makes me smile, because honestly? I'm prepared to say them back. When you know, you *know*.

Theo grabs my hand and starts leading me. "It's not a far walk, but when we get close, I'm going to need you to close your eyes."

My curiosity is skyrocketing, and I can't recall another time a woman went out of her way to not only surprise me with something like this but also make me close my eyes for it. I let her take the reins and drag me down the vacant sidewalk. Most of Chicago will surround their trees this morning, opening presents from Santa wrapped by loved ones and checking that the Big Guy ate the cookies and milk they left for him. But here Theo and I are, power-walking down State Street with light snow flurries kicking against our cheeks and eyelashes.

She stops us at a corner and turns to face me. "Okay, close your eyes, please."

"You're not going to lead me into traffic or something, are you?" I give her a sly grin.

She playfully rolls her eyes and makes a hurry-up gesture. "Of course not. You're far too valuable to me alive."

"Oh, good." A hearty chuckle roars from my belly, and I close my eyes but quickly pop one back open.

Theo squeals in defiance. "Axel, come on. Do *not* peek."

"I'm not, I'm not," I claim, still teasing her with half-closed eyes.

She groans, works her way behind me, and forces me to bend my knees to wrap her gloved hands over my eyes. "Okay, walk forward, you stubborn, handsome Viking, you."

Still smiling, I do as she's instructing and keep my arms outstretched in front of me like a zombie. "How far am I going?"

"Just a little further. Okay, here." A shaky breath flutters the back of my neck. "Ready?"

"Show me, Romance."

Her hands lift to reveal a quaint little corner of the city outfitted with red vendor stalls and elaborate holly, berries, and warm light garland hanging from the wooden scaffolding that borders the space. It looks familiar, yet slightly different.

"This is Christkindlmarket. A German holiday market festival. The city holds it every year, and I never thought to attend, but—" Theo slides in front of me, her fingers nervously playing against each other in front of her. "—I know this isn't Scandinavian per se, but I thought it might remind you a little of home? There's even mulled wine."

Her excitement to show me this has me so taken aback that I can't think of anything else but kissing her. I wrap my arms around her, pull her close, and kiss the ever-loving daylights out of her.

"Do you like?" She whispers once we pull away from the kiss, still wrapped in each other's arms.

"I can't think of a better way to spend Christmas day, Theo." I kiss the tip of her nose and wince at how cold it is before I cover it with my warm hand. "I'm surprised they're open."

She doesn't make a move to take my hand away. "I think the family that runs it celebrates *Jul*, too."

"What do you want to do first?" I ask, hugging her to my side and rubbing her arms through her jacket. It's not as cold today as it has been on Christmas day in the past in Chicago, but it's still chilly enough to numb my cheeks and make my nose tingly.

"This is your gift. What do you want to do, Axel?" Theo emphasizes her point by pressing a hand to my chest and patting twice.

Swiveling, I spy row after row of vendor stalls positioned directly beside each other, all with pointed tops like they're tiny houses. One displays the word *kaffee,* and despite it not being in English or Norsk, it's universal.

"How about some coffee? *I'm* feeling the temperature today, so I know you must be freezing." Chuckling, I continue to rub her arms, and she gives a firm nod of approval.

When we approach the stand, the worker, a man with a graying beard and a red knit cap slipped over his head, gives us a warm smile. "Merry Christmas," he says, leaning on the table separating us from him.

"Merry Christmas," I say back, eyes grazing the menu above him with only three options: black, peppermint, and vanilla.

"*God Jul,*" Theo says, surprising me.

The vendor slowly blinks at her behind his wire-rimmed glasses before slapping the table and offering a wide grin. "Well, that's something I haven't heard in quite some time, young lady. How's about your coffee's on the house? Consider it a Yule gift."

"Sir, you don't have to do that." Theo leans over the table, holding her hand up to fan back and forth.

"I insist. And tell you what? If you want to show support, check out my wife's stall three down from mine. She sells hand-crafted and painted ceramic mugs. Makes them herself from clay and all." The vendor flips two paper coffee cups into his hands, both designed elaborately with red and green holiday graphics.

Theo bites her bottom lip, looking to the mug stall in question and smiles. "Absolutely. Thank you so much, sir. I'll have peppermint, please."

In the spirit of things, I also order peppermint, and with paper cups secured with drinking lids, we loop our arms and take in the festival sights. A band comprised of a violin, flute, and accordion player has set up on a stage in the center. They play renditions *of I Saw Three Ships*, *Wassail, Wassail*, and *God Rest Ye Merry Gentlemen*.

Theo holds her phone up to me, showing the photo her parents text to her of them on a beach in Fiji. The palm trees in the background are decorated with green lights, and the two of them are smiling with streaks of sunscreen down their noses. Theo rests her head on my shoulder and holds her phone above us, snapping a selfie that she uses in her response to them.

We get to the coffee mug stall, and Theo's eyes light up. I imagined a dozen or so mugs, given the man told us she makes them by hand, but my jaw drops at the sight of *hundreds* of mugs in varying styles, colors, and sizes.

"These are beautiful," Theo says to the woman, her tight brown ringlets peppered with gray bouncing as she stands from a folding chair resting in the corner.

"Thank you kindly. We weren't sure how many customers we'd get today, given it's Christmas day and all, but I'm delighted to see a handful." The woman folds her hands behind her back, beaming at the merchandise on display in front of her and Theo perusing it with awe.

"Are you all closing early?" I ask, rubbing between Theo's shoulder blades as she makes the harrowing decision on which mug to buy.

"We are indeed. Want to be home in time for some ham dinner." The woman pats her belly and chuckles.

"I don't blame you." I smile at the woman, smells of my mother's glazed ham baking in the oven when I was a kid, anticipating how it'd make my mouth water while eating it, sprouting vividly in my mind given the familiar surroundings.

Theo picks a blue mug shaped like an elf shoe, a winter landscape with forests of snow-covered pine trees painted on the front and winding lights on the opposite side. We thank the woman and visit the rest of the shops, leaving with a decent-sized haul hanging from our arms in paper shopping bags—two pretzels to consume later, two heart-shaped cookies with pink frosting and words in German I didn't know, three hand-painted glass ornaments Theo wants to add to my tree, and several lighted paper stars that she wants to use to decorate her apartment.

Before we leave, I nudge Theo's arm and hand her my phone. "I need you to take a picture so I can text it to Spence."

"Is that why you're wearing the Santa hat?" Theo laughs and holds up my phone. "And here I thought you were being festive."

"Yeah, yeah. I lost a bet." Glancing around to make sure no one will see, I hold up my middle finger, flash a smug smile and Theo snaps a photo.

We're heading back to my apartment when Theo slides in front of me and takes both hands, the bags on her arms crinkling and swaying. "Before we head back, I have *one* more surprise."

"You're going to spoil me, Romance." I grin and kiss her. "And that's not a complaint."

She laughs, bubbly and bright, and leads me a block away. We're rounding a corner and arrive in a small patch of quaint homes still standing and surviving in the middle of the city. As lovely as the scenery is and how much this tiny chunk of suburbia surrounded by urban life is a sight, I'm confused *why* we're here.

"What's this all about?" One of my hands is on Theo and the other holds bags, so I point with my elbow.

She leans toward me and edges her chin at one of the front yards. "See the snow? It's the only piles I could find that haven't turned black and hard or have questionable yellow patches in them."

She looks so proud of herself, I choose my next words carefully. "Very nice. But, I'm still not fully following why we're…here?"

Theo rests the bags on the one dry spot on the sidewalk, urges me to do the same, and frolics to the snow, scooping some into her hands and beginning to form a ball.

Chuckling, I drop to my knees beside her, not caring when the cold wetness seeps through my jeans. "You want to build a snowman with me? In a stranger's front yard?"

"Yup," she answers, smiling as she pads more snow onto the ball. "There's not enough to make a full snowman, and I figured they're too occupied with Christmas festivities to notice us."

Glancing around us as if making a snowman with someone

else's snow could get us a misdemeanor, I shrug and start my own ball. We're a fit of laughs as we make our mini snowman, occasionally throwing snow at each other and constantly checking the windows or front door of the house. We've just put on the final touches with several black rocks and a twig for the snowman's bowtie when the door of the house creaks open. We don't wait long enough to know if the owners noticed us or if they were simply stepping outside, because we're scooping our bags into our hands, slipping and sliding on the sidewalk as we sprint away.

Theo manages to bring out this child-like side to me I thought had long since faded away. It's refreshing, nostalgic, and forces me to forget, but for those few moments, the responsibilities of writing and work. And it's precisely what I need. *She's* what I need—what I want.

We're back in my apartment, cold and wet. We hang our jackets near the fire to dry, and I slip my fingers into the top of her jeans, undoing the button, and working the zipper down.

"Trying to get me out of these clothes?" She grins, letting me do as I please.

"Always. But I'm going to throw them in the dryer." I wink at her, letting the tips of my fingers trail her skin as I drag the pants to her ankles. She steps out of them, one foot at a time, and soon shimmies to the fireplace in only a sweater and her blue lace panties. "Figured you might want lunch first. Especially when you see what I bought."

"Oh?" Theo has her palms open to the fire but arches a brow at me over one shoulder.

After throwing our jeans in the dryer, I return shirtless and in only my boxers, my stomach tightening when she does a double take of me. I remove the two truffle sandwiches I managed to procure the other day, undo the brown wrapping, and pop them in the toaster oven without saying a word.

Smells of mushroom, butter, and truffle soon fill the apartment as the sandwiches heat up. Theo drifts into the kitchen on her tiptoes like one of those cartoons where the character is mindlessly led to an apple pie chilling on the window sill by an animated scent line. She flattens her palms on the counter and flashes wide eyes at me. "Did you really?"

"I did." Smiling at her, I lean my back on the fridge and fold my arms. "And though they're delicious, maybe you can explain to me more in detail why you like them that much. Hm?"

"I don't think you're experiencing the individual flavors enough, Ax." Theo hops on a stool and taps her fingernails against the marble, impatiently waiting.

"Then, please do explain." I pluck one sandwich to a plate, the edge of it hotter than anticipated, burning my finger. "*Faen*," I curse under my breath.

Theo perks up. "What did you just say?"

I suck on my burnt finger, and rest the plate in front of her, gaze shifting from left to right. "*Faen*? It's a curse word."

Theo has yet to blink. "I've heard that before. Only I thought it was fawn or something." She gasps. "Were you at The Rooftop not that long ago?"

Using a towel to plate the other sandwich, I roll my shoulders and return to her. "Yeah. With Spence. Were you there too?"

Scents of vanilla, cinnamon and juniper…

"Do you believe in fate, Axel?" A warm smile brightens her face, and she lifts the sandwich to her lips with both hands.

"I think I do now." I sit on a stool beside her, ensuring our arms brush as we dig in, the perfectly toasted bread crunching under our teeth.

Theo lets out a sultry, sensual moan, and I pause before I choke on my food, taking a moment to watch her instead.

"Buttery toasted bread, caramelized portobello mushroom slivers, *Duke's* mayo laced with truffle extract, caramelized onions cooked in truffle oil, and thinly sliced flat iron steak cooked medium rare." Theo groans and takes another huge bite. "That's why I love this sandwich. You can't beat it."

I've suddenly lost my appetite. And not because I'm revolted by what she says or what she's doing, but because I'm far too preoccupied now with something else entirely.

"That thing you almost said earlier?" I wipe my fingers on a napkin, plucking it from the holder in the counter's center.

Theo tenses and covers her mouth with a hand as she finishes chewing. "What thing?"

Turning to face her, I pull her stool toward me so she's sitting between my legs. "If you repeat it, I may be inclined to say it back, Romance."

"But I—" She gulps the sandwich and turns to face me, her lips glossy from the butter, a speck of mayo collected at the corner of her mouth.

I lean my face into hers and kiss the mayo away.

"I—" Theo starts, her throat bobbing in a harsh gulp. "I love you, Ax."

"And I love you." The words come so easily that it feels like we've declared it a dozen times already.

Theo launches from the stool, wrapping her arms around me and smothering me with pecked kisses over my lips, my cheeks, her nose poking my eye at one point. A deep, rumbling chuckle escapes me, and I wrap my arms around her, nuzzling my nose against her neck.

"*Jeg elsker deg*, Theodora Hackett," I whisper to her.

Her head lifts, those emerald eyes filled with a glistening happiness that *I* put there. "*Jeg elsker deg*," she says back with flawless execution, as if she'd already been practicing. And just like that, this Viking finds his Shieldmaiden.

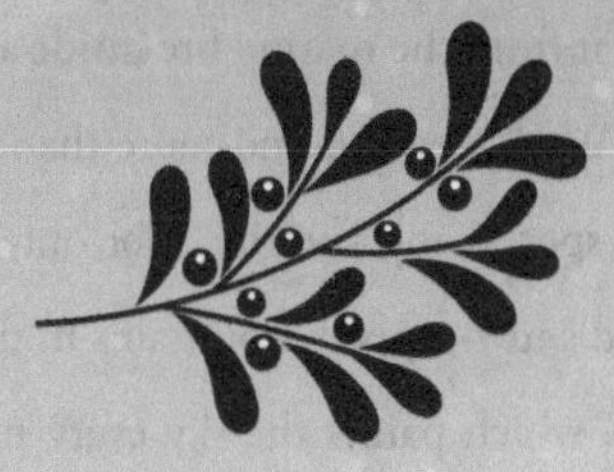

EPILOGUE

THEODORA

ONE YEAR LATER . . .
NORWAY

NOT ONLY IS this the first time I've traveled outside of the US in almost a decade it's also the first time I'm in Norway. And it's with *him*. My Viking. My everything. When he'd mentioned the idea several months ago to spend *Jul* in Norway and meet his family, I couldn't contain my excitement. And now that we're here? Postcards do not do this place justice. In any direction, you can see mountains, water, or snow-covered hills. The *fjords* we flew over upon arrival, with waterfalls, glaciers, and lakes literally took my breath away.

Axel booked us a quaint cabin on the lake's edge, allowing us to experience this beautiful country for ourselves for a couple of days before visiting his family. I'm sitting on the front porch, wrapped in a blanket, the heat from the roaring fire inside at my back from the propped door. We'd been here no more than thirty minutes, and I claimed this spot as my favorite. Not only because of the view of the lake and snow-capped mountains in the distance, but the aurora borealis, which paints the sky every night, morphing the scene into a surreal, animated painting.

The sun has set, and I'm sitting, waiting patiently for the light show to begin, when my phone starts ringing. It's Desiree asking to FaceTime, and I smile before swiping the screen and holding the phone up.

"Hey, Des," I say, my voice low, relaxed, and almost a little groggy.

It's loud wherever she is, pulsating music, chattering murmurs, and flashing lights.

"Hey, you. How's Viking Land?" Des rocks a shorter haircut now, and it suits her sassy personality, not to mention making her jawline sharp enough to cut glass.

"Amazing, but—" I stand, turning so that the mountain view is behind me and shown on camera. "—where are you?"

Desiree gasps and moves her face closer to the screen. "Look at that *view*. And oh, sorry, we're at Rupert's fashion show."

"Hi gorgeous," Rupert says, his face briefly appearing, and he flashes an exaggerated smile, his hand overenthusiastically waving.

"Hey, Rupy," I say with a chuckle. "Did you say *we*, by the way, Des?"

A mischievous glint forms in Desiree's eye. "Mmhm. Spence is here too." She turns the phone screen to a slumping Spencer, who jolts to attention and gives a tiny wave before slapping a hand over his face.

"Axel will never let him live this down." I bite my lip.

"Or you could not tell him," Spencer shouts from the background, but Desiree is already turning away, the phone pointed at her again.

"I know you have to, being that's our family dynamic, but don't go too harsh. He's being an absolute doll, keeping me company at this thing." Desiree's eyes pan to the left, clearly glancing at Spencer before looking back at me.

"Fair enough. I'm going to let you go now, though, okay? I heard Axel coming back inside from chopping wood." And it has my heart racing, antsy for his touch and warmth.

"He chops wood, too?" Rupert's eyes and nose peek from the corner of the screen.

Desiree playfully shoves him away by the face and blows me air kisses. "Have the best time, girly. We'll see you when you're stateside again."

After kissing my palm and holding it to the camera, I end the call in time for Axel to join me on the porch. He wears only a thin blue flannel shirt with rolled sleeves and a wool hat but slides it off and tosses it inside.

"Was that Desiree's voice I heard?" Axel's arms encircle me from behind, his chin resting on my shoulder, and he places a light kiss to my cheek.

"Yup. Checking in on me again. I swear, she's the doting big sister I never had." I purr against Axel's chest, leaning against him and wrapping my arms over his. "Spencer is with her and Rupert at a *fashion* show, by the way."

"Oh, yeah? He's never going to live that one down." His voice is a deep, rumbly, raspy vibration against my temple.

"That's what I said!"

Axel moves to my side and holds out his hand. "I tried to hurry up so I wouldn't miss the lights with you. Even started up the fire pit. Come on." He leads me to several fur-lined chairs surrounding a pile of overlapping wood blazing orange.

We sit next to each other, and I scoot my seat until it's flush with his, and I'm close enough to rest my head on his shoulder. Dark clouds move across the sky as the night dwindles, and eventually, they melt away, revealing black velvet littered with glittering dots in such massive clumps it lights the area around us in vibrant white. Bright green and blue streaks shimmer and sway as the northern lights greet us. I sit up, not daring to close my eyes for fear of missing even one second of nature's elaborate display. I can feel Axel's burning stare on my cheek. The first time he'd done this, I couldn't imagine why he would rather watch me over the lights, but I soon came to realize watching me become so joyous brought *him* joy.

"I'll never get tired of watching you continuously mesmerized by the world like discovering it for the first time," Axel says, his voice low and gritty near my neck.

Still smiling, my eyes glistening from tears over the beauty unfolding in the sky, I turn to him. "It makes me feel alive."

"And that's why I wanted to know if you'd like to meet my family with a different title other than my girlfriend." Axel's hand slips to my knee, squeezing it.

My heart is in my throat, trying to rationalize what he's talking about, and I tilt my head to one side. "What other title—" I start to say, but he's already kneeling on one knee in front of me.

"Theo—" He starts, removing a dark blue satin box from his pocket and holding it between us.

Tears immediately well up and surge down my cheeks, and I gasp, my hands flying to my mouth. "Yes," I yell, laughing and crying because I didn't let him finish.

Axel chuckles and hangs his head. "I'm ecstatic over your eagerness, but can I finish? Had this little speech prepared and—"

I kneel on the ground with him, running the lapels of his flannel through my fingers, sniffling, and trying to keep it together. "Yes. Please, yes. Go ahead."

"Despite how irritated I was being late for my first day of a new job because of this fiery redhead, I can truly say when I saw those emerald eyes smiling at me through the crack of the elevator doors, something sparked in me." The pad of his index finger rubs against the satin box. "I thought of a dozen different reasons for it, but now I know with every fiber of my being that spark was my heart telling my brain…*that's* your forever. And don't let her get away."

I'm in utter, blissful tears and doing nothing to stop them now. I don't even care that I'm probably making the "ugly crying face."

"So, I don't want to let you slip away, Romance." Axel opens the box, revealing a snowflake comprised of numerous tiny diamonds, a bigger one making up the center, and tiny sapphires bordering the design. "Will you do me the honor of becoming my wife, Theo?"

I've already said the word, but now it holds so much more impact, and I shout to the nothingness surrounding us, "Yes," so loudly it probably startles the polar bears in Svalbard. I cup his face in both hands and kiss each of his blonde eyebrows, the bridge of his nose, both cheeks, and finally land on his mouth. Grinning, he slips the ring onto my shaky finger, and I hold it up, astonished at how the aurora borealis sends rainbow shimmers bouncing off each stone.

"Theodora Nord," I whisper, my voice quivering from the excitement, nerves, and happiness. "I like the sound of that."

Axel answers with a radiant smile and sits by me on the grass near the firepit, grabbing my legs and draping them over his lap. He wraps his arms around me, letting me lay on his chest. And during this night of *Jul*, under the starry Norwegian skies, with the northern lights twinkling in joy over our union, I've become the *future—Mrs. Viking*.

Catch the first book in the Contemporary Mythos series:

HADES

The King of the Underworld may have found a woman
truly capable of melting his cold, dark heart.

HADES (Contemporary Mythos, #1)

BUY IT ON AMAZON

ACKNOWLEDGMENTS

FIRSTLY, TO MY HUSBAND, *my* Viking. I lent so much of us to these two characters and I'm so thankful to have moments with you for continued inspiration and can secretly share those instances with readers. I love you with all my Scandinavian heart!

To AK, I can't begin to say how much I appreciate your dedication to finishing this story in time to give honest and valuable feedback for me to make it the best I can in time for the holidays. And I know there's so much culture from this that you, too, could appreciate it and your enthusiasm makes me smile.

To Cerys and Morgana, for taking on this book last minute to alpha read and keep me honest, as well as finding those nabby plot holes!

To Shelby, thank you so much for whipping through last minute edits to help me find pesky typos and other things I'm so glad I had the chance to fix before publishing!

And finally, to my loyal readers, I appreciate you taking the chance on this contemporary romance from me when I realize I'm known for titles of a more fantastical variety. I hope you can find as much "magic" and still swoon your romance-loving hearts off with Axel and Theodora!

To the new readers, a sincere welcome and I hope this book

provides all the cozy holiday rom-com feels you probably picked up this book for. This vibe of feels, swoon, and banter is something you can always expect from me, even if mythological beings are involved.

STAY TUNED!
WWW.CARLYSPADE.COM

ABOUT THE AUTHOR

CARLY SPADE is an adult romance writer who has been writing since she could pick up a pencil. After the insanity of obtaining a bachelor's and master's degree in cybersecurity, creating worlds to escape to still ate at her very soul. She started writing FanFiction (which can still be found if you scour the internet), and soon felt the need to get her original ideas on paper. And so the adventure began.

She lives in Colorado with her husband and two fur babies, and revels in an enemies to lovers trope with a slow burn.

Find her online:
WWW.CARLYSPADE.COM